LITTLE BLACK CRIMES

CRIMES

Stories

Nathaniel Blackhelm

Close To The Bone Publishing

Contents

LITTLE BLACK CRIMES

The Lord saw that the wickedness of man was great in the earth, and that every intention of the thoughts of his heart was only evil continually.

—**Genesis 6:5**

.38 Special Kind of Love

He wasn't a boy. Let's get that straight. There was never any doubt in my mind. I've been with boys; been with men who felt like boys. Devonte wasn't anything like them. He was young, but he was already a man. He held me the way a man was supposed to. He loved me the way a man should. And I, in turn, gave him strength and lifted him up. I put the love of God into him whenever we touched.

It was there in our first touch, everything we needed to know. It was all laid out before us. Our paths and our pasts came together in an instant. Our stories and struggles melded into one. Mine was a chronicle of abuse by men; his, a history of family disappointments. These experiences became ours, no longer his or mine. He picked me up and we became the same.

"You're beautiful," he said. Those were his first words to me. Then he helped me out of the street where I lay. Joe Mullins had left me forsaken in the alley, after deciding he and I were through. That was Joe for you—Joe and every other man I'd ever known. Every time I helped them through a hard time, they would leave me back out in the cold.

But here was this new man, saving me from ruin. When he stroked me with his long and bony fingers, I felt a spark that heated me up. He looked at me with wonder in his widened eyes—those deep, dark, manly eyes. "Beautiful," he said. He pulled me close. Then he pressed me to his glorious lips.

On the way to his house, we got to talking. He seemed thrilled to be able to speak from the heart. He talked fast, hardly taking a breath between sentences as he guided us down the back streets and alleyways. He kept his coat draped around me the entire time we walked together. Such a gentleman. I could feel myself falling for him already. I longed to hear him talk about his life.

He told me about the only life he liked: the life he lived inside. He said there were pictures he drew in his head, and sometimes on paper, of the things that had been denied him. A mother. A father. Someone other than his grandmother to talk to. He said most people had been scared away when he would speak of the holes in his life. But I was different; he could already tell. I was listening, whereas others had turned away.

"You don't think I'm crazy?" he asked. "I can't believe you don't think I'm crazy. Maybe it's because you don't know me yet. My grandmother definitely thinks I'm crazy."

Devonte told me about this woman—his father's mother—who had raised him from the time he was an infant. His parents had abandoned him to her for reasons she had never fully explained, beyond calling it *the will of the Lord*, or *the Lord working in mysterious ways*, or *the Lord having given just as He had taken away*, as if any of those clichés could help a young boy understand the true circumstances of his existence. As he'd gotten older, his questions had become more insistent, until she had finally been forced to surrender at least a version of the truth: his father had been a runaway drug addict, and his mother had vanished without a trace. But that was all he could get from the old and tired woman. Pressed further, she would answer the way she answered all of life's questions: with passages recited from the Bible.

She had forced Devonte to read such passages aloud from an early age. He didn't like the stories, just the sound of the words as they passed through his lips—that certain inexplicable strength he felt in his voice as he read them aloud. But he wouldn't become a preacher like his grandmother wanted. He didn't believe in God enough to stand in front of a congregation, speaking of glories he'd never bought into or riches that had never come his way. All he really had to talk about was the anger he felt and the fantasies in his head about punishing the ones in his life who had wronged him. He said revenge was constantly on his mind.

"When I was seven," he said, "I drew a picture of my family. My mother was a tiger and my father was a lion and they had eaten all their babies but me. But when they tried to eat me, my mouth opened big and I ate them instead." Devonte paused to make sure the street was clear. "I don't know where that picture went. Maybe I never even drew it. But it's always stayed in my head."

I wasn't used to being confided in this way. Most of the men whose company I had shared had been the strong and silent types who avoided getting personal. No matter how much I would do for them, no matter how long we were together, they would never really bare their souls to me. But Devonte had no such reservations. When he told me how little experience he had, I could hardly believe it; I had certainly been fooled by his commanding touch. Nowhere were the sweaty hands or any of the usual symptoms of a man who didn't know what he was doing. He had made me feel completely comfortable in his presence, made it so I didn't want to leave his side. I couldn't remember a time when someone felt so right. I was fine with going home with him this early.

Devonte lived in an old two-story row house. His grandmother wasn't around when we arrived. We climbed the stairs swiftly to his room. Once inside, he shut the door behind us and locked it.

The walls of his room were plastered with drawings, the two largest being a tiger and a lion hanging side by side. The two animals faced each other, a trail of blood dripping from the lion's mouth. On a mirrored dresser lay a pen and sketchpad, its pages open to a half-finished drawing of what appeared to be a man with a spear. A hoodie lay next to the sketchpad. To one side of the room was a closet; to the other side of the room, a nightstand and bed.

It was there, upon the bed, where Devonte first lay me down, giving me the same look of wonder he had given me on the street. It made me feel glorious inside. I hadn't been looked at like that in ages. Here was a man who recognized my splendor, who didn't look on me with jaded eyes. My beauty had been squandered so long amongst thieves, I had forgotten that I had once been captivating. He pulled me up and held me—close, so close. I brushed against his face and hair. Then he looked at our reflection with tears in his eyes. He caressed me till I felt I might explode.

A hum of voices rose from outside. Then came a knock at the door.

"Devonte?" called an old woman's voice.

Devonte's panicked eyes scanned the room for a place to hide me. He bent down and lifted up the bed skirt. Down there was our only hope: there looked to be enough room for me to fit underneath. I slid under the bed on the cold, wooden floor. He released the bed skirt when I was all the way under.

"Devonte?" came the voice again, more insistent. The handle of the door rattled.

"Yes, grandma?" he said.

"Are you ready for your home visit? Miss Whitney is here to see you."

"One second!" He peeked under the bed one more time to make sure I was fully concealed. Then I heard his footsteps move toward the door. The lock turned and the door opened and the voice of Devonte's grandmother filled the room:

"What were you doing in here? What have I told you about locking your door?"

"It's okay, Mrs. Henderson," came a younger female voice. "I'll take it from here."

Her footsteps entered the room, making a *clop clop clop* on the wooden floor.

"Hello, Devonte. How are you today?"

"Alive," he mumbled.

"Are you two going to be okay?" called Devonte's grandmother from down the hall. "I'm going downstairs to fix dinner."

"We're fine," said the female. "I'll leave the door open, Mrs. Henderson." Her steps clopped closer and she sat beside Devonte on the bed, making it squeak. "Have you had a good week?"

"Nothing special."

"Anything in particular happ—"

"Did you do what I asked?" he interrupted.

"You first," she said. "Got anything new to show me?"

"Mm-hmm."

The bed skirt ruffled and an upside-down hand, Devonte's hand (for those long and bony fingers could only be his), swept this way and that in front of me until it brushed against the handle of a backpack and dragged it out from under the bed. A zipper unzipped and I could hear him rummaging through his school things.

"It's *somewhere* in here," he said. Then the flap of a sheet of paper being withdrawn. "*Here* it is."

"Let's see," she said. "Oh, nice. Looks like you got a 'smiley face' on this. Do you mind if I read it?"

"I don't care."

"I remember these. It's a haiku, right?"

"Mm-hmm."

Her voice began: "*I am a hunter. / I eat lions for breakfast, / And tigers for lunch*. I like it," she said. "But what do you eat for dinn—"

"Did you do it for me or not?"

She clicked her tongue. "Look Devonte, about that…"

A clanging of pots and pans could be heard from downstairs. The female sighed. "I wish I could help you. I really do. But I don't think we're quite there yet in terms of our progress."

"What do you mean? I've been doing what I'm supposed to, right?"

"Lately, yes." She shifted off the bed. Her feet double-clopped onto the floor. "If only that was enough."

"What does *that* mean?"

"Look, I can't do this. I can't help you anymore."

"Huh?"

"I'm sorry. But this is over. I've tried my best."

Devonte stood up. "Wait a minute. What's going on?"

"I should have told you this earlier. I won't be working with you anymore after today."

"*What?* Why?"

"I'm having you reassigned to a different home-based counselor. Someone better qualified to help you out."

"No, please. That can't happen. My grandmother will throw me out. She said if it didn't work out with you, that'd be the last straw."

"It's okay, I'll explain it to her. It's just a transfer.

You'll be working with someone other than me from now on, that's all."

"But she won't understand," he said. "She's a stupid old lady and she won't understand."

"I'm sure that's not true. I'll do my best to explain it to her."

"It won't work. I'll be gone by tomorrow. *Please.*"

Something crashed to the floor downstairs.

The female took a deep breath. She started over in a softened voice.

"You know what, Devonte? You've been lied to enough in your life. So let me tell you what's really going on here. It's *me* who messed up, not you. I should have never agreed to do you that favor. I stupidly thought that if I could find him for you, it'd be a good thing. That you could write to him or someth—"

"So you found him?"

"Uh," she hesitated. "No, I didn't say that. All I can say is I never should have stuck my nose in where it didn't belong. I overstepped big time. For someone like me, there's no going back from that."

"You found him, didn't you? But there's something about him that must have scared you."

She rustled nervously through her things. "I thought I had a notepad in here. I need to leave you my replacement's contact info."

"Is my father near here? Sometimes I feel like he's near."

"Tell you what, I'll just write on the back of your haiku if that's okay."

"What about my mother? Did you find her too?"

She clopped over to the dresser. "Mind if I borrow this pen?" There was a scribbling sound as she wrote.

"Why aren't you answering me?" he demanded.

She tore off a piece of the paper and handed it to him. "Don't lose this. It's just for you. Are you listening, Devonte? *Just for you.*"

"I'll bet you found them. You must have."

"Look, I've gotta go."

"You going downstairs to tell my grandmother now?"

She nodded.

"*Don't,*" he said.

She clopped toward the door. "Take care of yourself, Devonte. And please know I'm sorry for everything."

"You *will* be," he muttered under his breath. The female continued down the hall. Devonte dropped to the floor. His arm punched through the bed skirt to reach for me.

"I almost forgot," she said, announcing her return. He gasped and quickly withdrew his hand. The bed skirt ruffled and blew in a gust of air, sucking in the torn sheet of paper. "I'd hate to steal the pen of such a great artist." She handed him the pen. "And remember, whoever gave you that piece of paper… it wasn't me."

Her footsteps retreated down the hall. Once she was downstairs, her voice rose faintly. Devonte listened from the hallway. There was the young female voice, then the old. The old, then the young. Then their voices began to intermingle. The old voice clipped the young one off several times until only the old voice remained, shouting: "Don't nobody know how much I've suffered! Don't you or nobody else!"

The young voice came back, too quiet to hear. A distant clopping, then the slam of a door. Devonte was low again in no time, peeling up the bed skirt. The torn sheet of paper caught his eye in the light. On it was scrawled:

Lionel Henderson
1046 Church St.
Apt. 403

Devonte's fingers caught the end of the scrap.

"I *knew* it!" he said with a shaking voice. "I *knew* she found him!" Sure enough, she had come through for him. "This isn't that far away!"

The old woman's voice boomed from downstairs. "Young man, we need to talk!"

"Shhhit." He rose and went down the stairs to meet his fate. Soon the voices began to rise from the kitchen. The old woman's voice smothered Devonte's. Then Devonte's became the voice of a preacher—passionate, vibrant, irresistibly hypnotic—as he read what must have been passages from the Bible aloud.

A set of footsteps entered the room. I heard a drawer open, the sound of rummaging, then the drawer close. The sequence repeated itself as another drawer opened and closed. The footsteps shuffled deeper into the room. A doorknob turned and the closet door swung open, releasing a small rubber ball that bounced several times before invading my space under the bed. It had come to a halt just in front of me.

"I'll find them somewhere," came the old woman's voice from inside the closet. There was rustling, clattering, the sound of things being lifted and rearranged. She made a straining sound as something tumbled and fell heavily to the ground, spreading its contents across the floor. The top half of a basketball card peeked its way under the bed skirt. The old woman cursed. I could hear her withdrawing from the closet. Then the card vanished from my sight. A set of thin, wrinkly fingers swept back and forth where the card had been. They looped under the bed skirt and began to draw it up.

"What are you doing?" came Devonte's voice from the doorway. His grandmother's fingers dropped the bed skirt.

"Jesus!" she said. "You scared me half to death! You supposed to be reading, young man."

"Why are you in my room? Why were you looking under there? Why is my closet open?"

"I'm looking for your drugs. Where you hiding 'em?"

"Drugs? You think I'm on drugs?!"

"I *know* you are," she said. "I know it from your father before you. This business with Miss Whitney wouldn't have happened no other way."

"That's not true! It's not my fault she won't be seeing me anymore! You don't under—"

"Don't raise your voice to me, young man. I have suffered like you don't know. Don't nobody know how much I've suffered."

"Nobody cares," said Devonte. "Nobody cares about your worthless life. I'm so sick of hearing—"

There was the sound of a slap.

"I raised you, boy," barked his grandmother. "You don't talk to me like that."

"Do it again," said Devonte through gritted teeth. "I dare you to do it again."

There was the sound of another slap, this time harder.

"I'll do it till you straighten up," she said. "I couldn't straighten up your father, but I will damn sure set you straight."

I heard a roar like an animal. There was the quick shuffle of footsteps, an animal's charge. Then I heard his grandmother cry out in pain as her body crashed hard against the nightstand. She wailed a miserable wail of defeat.

Devonte stood over her, breathing heavily.

"Oh, grandma. Why did you make me do that?" She was moaning and sobbing on the floor. Devonte began sobbing, too. "I can't ever come back now, can I? There's no coming back here for me. Isn't that what you told me? That if I ever laid a hand on you, there'd be no coming back?"

"Just like your father. Damn right you won't never come back."

"Then I guess this is goodbye."

I saw his hand pull up the bed skirt, saw his face down against the floor, his teary, desperate eyes staring in at me. No more waiting, then. It was finally going to happen. His hand shot past the rubber ball until I was finally back in his grasp.

"That where you keeping 'em?" his grandmother said. "I should have known to check under the bed."

"You shut up. If you're smart, you'll shut your mouth." He helped me out from under the bed and lifted me up as he got to his feet. There we stood, as a couple, before her. Devonte was still sobbing, but I smiled my prettiest smile. He grew calmer as we stood there together, watching his grandmother's eyes fill with genuine terror.

"Oh dear Jesus," she pleaded, raising her hands to cover her face. "Oh dear Lord, Devonte, don't."

Devonte towered over her, aiming my barrel down at her head. His finger rested lightly on my trigger. "I don't like drugs," he said. "I don't do drugs. Never have, never will."

"Oh but Devonte, please, I didn't mean it…"

"I don't need drugs to think the way I think."

"Devonte, oh Devonte… remember what we read…"

"Do. You. Understand?"

"Yes, oh yes, I understand, please," she said, peeking

through her arms. "You don't need drugs." The floor was getting wet, and a foul smell was filling the room.

"As you can see, I am a hunter. I eat lions for breakfast, and tigers for lunch."

"Lions for lunch, yes," she said. "'For a living dog is better than a dead lion.' Remember what we read? 'The living know they will die, but the dead know nothing… they have no more reward, and even the *memory* of them is lost. Their love and their hate and their envy have already perished. And never, *never* again will they have any share in all that happens under the sun.' Do you know what that means, Devonte?"

"That *dead* is forever. I know you don't deserve to die." Her eyes grew less terrified. "I remember reading that out loud to you," he said. "I never knew what it meant. It was one of the first things you made me read. 'A living dog is better than a dead lion,'" he repeated. "Seems to me that we're the living dogs. And no better than the lion, unless he's dead."

Devonte picked up his hoodie from the dresser. "I'm going to find your son," he said.

I heard his grandmother muttering something as we left her in the room: "'You are not able to go against this Philistine to fight with him… for you are just a boy and he has been a warrior from his youth…'"

I don't know if Devonte heard her, but she was wrong. She hadn't come to know him like I had. For if there was one thing I was sure of, it was this: I was leaving in the company of a *man*.

So you know by now what I am. You know what I was made for, you know what I am used for, you know what things I normally do. And knowing these things, you can hopefully understand why I couldn't introduce myself to you by name from the start. When Devonte called me beautiful, you wouldn't have bought it. When I told you we were in love, you would have laughed. You would have likely held certain prejudices against me—and then you wouldn't have bothered hearing me out.

Everyone needs someone to hear them out.

Even a .38 Special like me.

And we ran through the streets, hand in handle, heart to heart. We moved like a well-oiled machine. Over and under, sideways and in-between, through jungles of concrete and shrubbery. With me in his right hand, the torn sheet of paper in his left, Devonte carried us over to Church Street. There was fear in his heart, and I could feel it all the way. The remorse was even greater than the fear. He kept talking about what he had done to his grandmother, panting *I'm sorry, I'm sorry, I'm sorry* as he ran.

I felt myself slipping away from him, disconnecting, then I would cycle back and feel close to him again. He would close up and open, close up and open, and I reminded him that we were best when we were sharing our hearts. The rhythm of his running, the pattern of his breath, I tried my best to pantomime, keeping pace with the passing terrains, sending messages so soothing to his palm, his sex, his every vital organ, which belonged to me as much as to him.

Come back to me, I commanded, and I brought his mind back to stay. I reminded him that together, we were more than the sum of our parts. *You are more than man and I am more than machine, and neither one of us needs remorse. What's done is done, our lives are in front of us. Let's find our sunset and melt into one. One is how we met, one is what we have not yet strayed from. Come back to me, return to us.*

And as he did, his breathing slowed and he moved

again with certainty, shedding fears through his sweating pores. Remorse made a crater when he dropped it behind him, a black hole for a rabbit to find. We were moving so fast now, over *who-knows-what* terrain, asking *where-the-hell-are-we?*, but never doubting. Grove became roadway, wooded path became boulevard, and we were gliding overtop of it all.

Then the compound came into view, the enemy stronghold. The apartment complex wherein our prey resided. He was in there right now, doing God-knows-what. He was a *God-knows-who* kind of person. In our oneness, our togetherness, we could sense him moving around. He was pacing like a lion in a cage. Watching us, maybe. Sensing us, perhaps. But he had never been hunted like this.

We pulled our hood over our head and watched the complex from behind the chain link fence. We waited for the humming of the night to tell us that our prey had temporarily looked away. *He is no longer watching, go now,* the night hummed. *You only have a second to move.*

And we did, not even feeling our feet climb the fence. We might have even slipped through its diamond-shaped openings. We ourselves were like a hole, invisible as we floated, teleporting without transmitting our image. We might have scaled the walls like a climbing panther, or leapt several floors at a time. We did something to end up on the open-air staircase four floors above without having dropped from the fence. And the Lion had not detected us. We could feel that he had been looking away. If those were his underlings surrounding the building, they too had failed to notice our flight.

The Lion's Den stood unguarded. It was the apartment door that matched the address. To breach it, we would have to use the tear on the paper, the makeshift knife of its ripped edge. We raised it to the doorknob and began to saw, sawing quietly, as quietly as we could. Once the doorknob was severed, it dropped with a *tink*. Then we raised our foot and kicked in the door.

Things, people, insects scattered. They all rushed past us, pushing us back. *But forward. We must go forward. The Lion now knows we're here to make him extinct.*

Our grandmother's voice came back into our heads. "Don't nobody know how much I've suffered." *Remorse. Remember? Remorse. What did we do to her?*

"What did I do to her?" Devonte said out loud. It was too late for me to pull him back. We were two again, separate, in this of all places, the dreaded Lion's Den. Two, not one. An object and a man. A gun in a baby's hand.

"Who the hell are you?" said the Lion-Man to Devonte, aiming his gun at Devonte's head. Devonte was aiming me back at his father. Behind us, the kicked-in door of the apartment was halfway open.

"You first," said Devonte. His hands were shaking. "Who the hell are *you*?"

"No one to you," said the Lion-Man.

"The hell you aren't."

"What, you got some bad shit from me? I fuck you over or something?"

"Oh, you fucked me over alright." Devonte gripped me as tight as he could, trying to steady his hands.

"Well, maybe we can talk this over, kid," said the Lion-Man. "I'm a reasonable kind of guy."

"And I'm a guy with no reason to believe you."

"Ain't you young to hold such a grudge? The fuck I do to you?"

"You must have done something to make my life shit. I'm trying to figure it out."

"You're a crazy sumbitch, ain't ya? Ain't quite got your head on straight."

"Fuck you. You wouldn't know a goddamned thing

about my head."

"Whoa ho ho," laughed the Lion-Man. "You the craziest damn kid I ever seen. But kid or no kid…" His face became a face like a lion's in an instant. "For threatening me, you're gonna pay with your life."

"No need. I've got that covered." Devonte placed me against his own temple. "But first, you should know who I am."

"I couldn't care less," said the Lion-Man. "You crazy sumbitch. Go on and do it already."

Something behind the Lion-Man caught Devonte's eye.

"That picture over there," Devonte said. "The one on the refrigerator. Who made it?"

The Lion-Man turned to look. "What pic—"

Devonte aimed me forward and squeezed me again and then again. I screamed and screamed as I came all over the Lion-Man. Tremors, aftershocks moved through my system. It had been so long since I had come. Just feeling Devonte's touch made me want to come again.

The smoke cleared in front of me and I could see a hole in each of the Lion-Man's shoulders. He had dropped his gun, firing once into the ground before staggering back into a seated position on the couch. The red was beginning to leak from his holes. Devonte was breathing even more heavily than his victim. He kept me pointed at the Lion-Man.

"N-now we can talk," Devonte said.

A slow smile formed on the Lion-Man's face. He let out as much of a laugh as he could muster. "Good one. You got me good."

"When I was seven," said Devonte, "I drew a picture of my family. My mother was a tiger and you were a lion and you had eaten all your babies but me. But when you tried to eat me, my mouth opened big and I ate you instead."

The Lion-Man scoffed. "The fuck does that have to do with me?"

"You know that picture you looked for that wasn't behind you? That was it."

The Lion-Man leaned forward, groaning.

"You know why it wasn't there?" asked Devonte.

"Enlighten me," said the Lion-Man, collapsing back into the seat.

"Cuz I just now made it for you to see. Look closely. Look at me. Tell me who you see."

"A crazy sumbitch even crazier than me."

"That's right. Now answer the question. You know who I am, so tell me."

"Me. Is that who you're supposed to be? You're me."

"Close. But we're running out of time. So why don't I just go ahead and spoil it for you?"

The Lion-Man's white t-shirt was now completely red. His eyes were growing heavy.

"Your mother raised me," said Devonte. "She made me read the Bible out loud every night. Did she make you do that too?"

"The fuck…?" The Lion-Man perched himself up, a spark of wonderment in his animal eyes.

"Don't pretend to care," said Devonte. "It makes this harder to do."

"Wait a second. What's your name?"

"Devonte."

"*Devonte.* That's right. I told her to name you Jacob," said the Lion-Man. "But your mama, she wasn't into that biblical shit."

"What do you know about my mother?" Devonte lowered me to his side.

"Your mama? Oh I knew her *very* well. In the biblical sense of *knowing*," the Lion-Man chuckled. "As a person?

Not so much. Shame for you and me both she didn't just stick to swallowing."

Devonte raised me again. "Don't talk about my mother like that."

"You didn't even know her. That's just the way she was."

Devonte took a step forward, gripping me tighter.

"First time I fucked her, she wasn't even conscious," said the Lion-Man. "She was all partied-out. Damn, that bitch could party."

I could feel Devonte's finger adding weight to my trigger. I wanted so badly to come again.

"For all I know, that was the time she got pregnant," said the Lion-Man. "So there's your origin story for you."

Devonte took another step forward. "Why didn't she raise me?"

"That part ain't on me, kid. So don't be putting that on me. She came in here with all these demands after you were born. Wanted money and a car, and threatened to—"

"To what?"

"No one threatens *me*," said the Lion-Man.

"What happened to her *then*?"

The Lion-Man was silent. Sirens were approaching in the distance.

"What happened to her *then*, I said?!"

"What. Do you. Think?"

"Say it. I want to hear you tell me what you did."

"Jesus, kid. Why make it painful?"

"Why *not*? Thanks to you, that's how it's always been."

"Christ! Don't put that on me. I made it easy on her, okay? That's all you need to know. Then I left you in your grandma's hands." He laughed a hopeless laugh. "The old self-righteous, Jesus freak cunt…"

Devonte took a final step forward. "Why should I have mercy on you?" *That's it. Finish me. I can only come one more time.*

"Luke 6:36," said the Lion-Man. "'Be merciful, just as your father is merciful.'"

"I have no father," Devonte said.

He squeezed my trigger and I screamed and came all over the Lion-Man's face.

The smoke cleared as I was shuddering and I found myself against Devonte's hair, remembering when he had held me like this in his room, remembering our reflection in the mirror and the tears that had filled his eyes. For the first time all day, I started to think of our fates as separate, for now that I was spent, we could do no more good for each other. Still he tried, squeezing my trigger again and again as he held me against his head, screaming at me to perform the impossible. But it was impossible. *Impossible.* Impossible that he threw me down, threw me across the room like I was nothing to him—like I had never meant anything to him at all.

He finally, and I hate remembering this part, finally took three steps back and dropped to his knees, crawling to the place where his father had dropped a double, a device that looked and worked like me but didn't have the same soul or memories. My insides sank as he held it in his mouth, not wanting to see him share those pleasures, not wanting to see him unfaithful in the least, but it was impossible *not* to see, impossible *not* to hear the terrible scream it made as he made it come into his mouth.

And like that, it was over. Everything we'd had was gone. Of all the cold places I had ever been left alone, that room was the coldest of all.

***

At least it's not cold where I'm spending my days now. Just utterly boring. In here, I have nothing but memories. There is no one to talk to, nothing to see—save the pictures inside my head.

I've been trying to piece together our sad little story. Not much else to do in a sealed evidence bag.

Devonte and me were something else. I'll stay true to him as long as I can.

The Misconception

I. Body Politic

Adam was ready to take his own life; but not before leaving life behind. In new life, after all, there would be new hope— hope to be reborn, beautiful and right this time, through another incarnation of the self. But a willing reproductive partner was out of the question: any potential child-bearers had always retreated from him. It was as if they could sense the flaws of his gene pool, the madness of his sordid line. It was a line in which Adam was the last. His mother and father had been sister and brother; they had hanged themselves, without leaving him a sibling. Without a sister for a mate, or a willing partner, there was only one option that remained.

The abduction and impregnation of a random, fertile female.

But a barrier in his mind had always kept him from that. It was a barrier of morality that reined him in, preventing him from attempting such a crime—a crime the only thing sicker than which was the thought of the nothingness that would await him beyond death. If he died without planting his seed, there would be no vessel through which any parts of him could continue. No way to remain in this world in any form once he had ended his own existence. He would simply cease to be after committing suicide.

For years, he weighed the terror of that thought against the prospect of abducting and forcibly impregnating a female subject. He leaned heavily toward the crime, but one crucial unknown had always damned him to stagnancy: the uncertainty of whether the unwilling child-bearer would simply terminate the pregnancy, killing his seed and any hope of a better version of himself being born. But then, one morning, the world around him finished wrapping up a pretty little gift it had been working on for quite some time.

The night had been its usual ordeal, filled with dreams of birth and death, fetuses and nooses. Then something awoke him from his sleep, from the slumber of his stagnated existence. It ripped a line through his brain, no longer just a sound, but a feeling taking hold of his face. The sound had emanated, and now echoed, from the flickering screen in the corner of the room that had been lighting the space of Adam's basement-level apartment during the previous few weeks of statewide political commotion. The voice of the newscaster repeated a line in an endless loop, though it was probably just a glitch in her cognition, or maybe the teleprompter she was reading from, or maybe the station's broadcast signal, or maybe Adam's TV, or maybe existence itself:

"…as the statewide ban on abortions at any point after conception went into effect this morning… as the statewide ban on abortions at any point after conception went effect this morning… as the statewide ban on abortions at any point after conception went into effect this morning…"

Adam accepted the pronouncement for what it was, and what he had been waiting for. It lifted him from the place on the floor he had surrendered consciousness either years earlier or just the night before—the *when* of it didn't matter, just the fact that he was moving *now*. He rushed to the bathroom to see the new face the sound had unleashed. A crack. A crack. A crack was in the mirror. The same crack that had always made his image more tolerable. Yet there was also now a crack behind his eyes. He could feel it without seeing it. There, in the space where the barrier had once stood, a light shone through upon its rubble. And in his new reflection, an obscene smile of life formed upon his lips.

He could do it now. He could more than just picture it. There was no more doubt in his mind. With the world around him changed—and no more barriers in place to stop him—he could finally plant his seed and leave the world.

II. Bodies on the Runway

At the annual junior fashion show extravaganza in the mall, young bodies were on display: some childlike; some more expectedly adolescent; and then there was Ebony's—the one that stood out in the crowd. Her ungodly proportions had the audience captivated, but also completely fooled: given to guessing, most would have assumed she was of legal age. Yet like Mari—her best friend since elementary school, who was watching from the crowd—she was only fourteen.

"Yo, that's my girl," said Jamal, poking Mari in the ribs. "That's my shit up there." Ebony strutted to the end of the runway, stared intensely into the distance, and turned around. "There go the best part," Jamal announced as his girl's shapely ass swayed to and fro. Mari felt the hopelessly flat surface where the backs of her legs came together. She ached with envy watching Ebony descend the stairs of the runway.

"Bring her back," called Jamal. "Bring back that lovely back." All eyes were on him now that Ebony had left the stage, his crude cheerleading drawing attention to how much older he looked than the girl he was hyping. Like the crowd, he too had once been fooled by Ebony's appearance, though discovering her real age—a full decade less than his own—hadn't given him much pause. A perfect build was a perfect build, statutory laws be damned. As for Ebony, dating a man who had lived almost a quarter of a century was a no-brainer. She had happily skipped the middle and high school dating pools for the water park thrills of a way older guy.

A new song came on, less provocative than the last. The next junior model looked her age. She reminded Mari of herself, though she thought herself fatter, and nowhere near as pretty in the face. Mari imagined the song they would play were she herself on the runway—a song from her nightly exercise playlist. She imagined the eyes all over her, the stares she had earned, from working so hard to stay thin. The funny, if not cruel part, was how much harder she worked at it than any of these girls—especially Ebony. Whenever Mari would ask her friend what she did to keep in shape, the answer was always the same: "Not a damn thing. It's just the genes my mama gave me."

It was maddening.

Mari would never go a single night without exercising; any less than four hours was a sin. And she had systematically forsaken all fatty foods over the course of the past few months. She was ashamed for all the normal foods she had eaten earlier in the year—that simpler time before her declaration of war against every last ounce of fat in her system. But at least she was making up for it now. This week had been a major victory so far: she hadn't eaten a single bite in three days.

The streak continued as she sat across from Ebony and Jamal in the food court during an intermission in the fashion show. It was both joy and misery to watch them devour their burgers while trying to remember the taste of fast food. She was savoring their every chew, till Jamal gave them something else to swallow.

"Better eat up," he told Ebony, stuffing his burger in his mouth. "Don't forget you eating for two now."

"Jamal!" Ebony shrieked. Her hands went up to cover her face.

"Oh shit," he said, looking at Mari. "I forgot she won't supposed to know."

Mari felt a chill run through her. Ebony kept her hands over her face.

"Damn, baby," Jamal said. "It was an accident."

Ebony's face slowly emerged. She met eyes with

Mari. "Yes, it was."

Mari didn't know what to say. All she could think of was the weight Ebony would gain. The thought of it made her morbidly happy. After all this time, she might finally have the better body for a while.

"Please don't tell my mom," Ebony said.

"Don't worry," Mari assured her.

"Yeah, don't worry, baby," Jamal chimed in. "I know all about this. You gonna make a beautiful mama."

"You talking like I've made up my mind."

"What, you *haven't*?"

"Can you please just shut up?!"

"Oh baby, calm down, I'm sorry." Jamal reached for Ebony's cheek, but she slapped it away. He got up to calm her down and they started playfighting. After a few fake blows, they started swapping spit as if no one was around. Ebony pulled away from their make out session when she noticed her friend staring at something in the distance.

"Mari?"

Mari heard the blurred sound of her name being called. It broke her focus on the man standing by the column—the man she had noticed looking her way. "Hmm?" she said.

"Where were you?"

"Oh, sorry."

"Who you lookin' at over there?" said Jamal. He turned his head to scan the crowd in the food court. Mari looked too, but the man by the column was gone.

"Yeah, which one you like?" said Ebony. "Want me to go up to him?"

"No, no," Mari said. "I was just staring into space. Just thinking."

"Mm-hmm," said Ebony playfully.

"'Bout time to get back to the show," said Jamal,

checking his watch. "Now that Victoria's Secret is out, we'd best be going."

"You crazy," said Ebony.

"For you," said Jamal. The two of them rose with their trays. Mari rose after them, lightheaded. This happened sometimes; it would usually pass within seconds. She grasped the top of the chair to steady herself. Once the stars in front of her eyes had cleared, she saw the man who had been staring receding down the corridor that led to the bathrooms.

Ebony and Jamal returned from dumping their trays.

"Ready?" Ebony asked.

"Just have to pee first," Mari said.

"Okay. Just find Jamal in the crowd."

The trio parted ways.

Mari was glad she wasn't walking with them. She needed some time to herself to think. After all, it was a lot to stomach: Ebony was pregnant. The same Ebony she had idolized so much this past year, in her secret quest to emulate her body. Mari had walked beside her in the halls of the middle school, studying her every gesture, trying to copy her every movement, so as to burn the same number of calories, to somehow near—even in the smallest imaginable way— that impossible standard of perfection embodied in her friend. Yet now Ebony had gone and done something impossible to emulate: gotten herself pregnant. Two months with this older guy and she was already carrying his child. Which meant she would have had to...

"Fuck!" yelled a lady who collided with Mari in the corridor. "Watch where you're going!"

"Sorry! I didn't see you."

"Obviously," said the woman, who was wearing a *Life Begins at Conception* t-shirt. She stormed away with a hateful scowl.

"What is it with people nowadays?" came a voice by

the bathrooms. Mari realized it was the man who had been staring at her in the food court. As he approached, she saw that he was an older man, even older than Jamal—but rougher than him, less handsome. Something about the structure of his face looked… *off*. His eyes gave her a strange feeling.

"Every time I come out, I'm reminded why I never leave the house," he said.

She saw his gaze fixed on the cross around her neck. His eyes lowered to appraise the rest of her. She took a step back.

"Stranger danger," he said. "I get it."

Mari was anxious for someone else to come down the corridor.

"Forgive me for being so forward, I just haven't talked to anyone in ages. A *normal* conversation."

"I'm sorry," she said. "Sorry to hear that."

"Don't be silly." He smiled an odd kind of smile. "It's a sign of the times. We're all so isolated nowadays. Everyone strung up on their own personal crosses."

She saw a flash of herself strung up on a cross, like the figure on her necklace.

"Anyways, I owe you an apology," he said.

"For what?"

"I think you know."

She didn't respond, though she thought she might know what he meant.

"For what happened in the food court. See, I have this bad habit of staring at beautiful girls." He smiled a gentle smile, his eyes holding hers; they looked younger now, less terrifying. She narrowed her eyes, as if puzzling over his words.

"I think you're something else. Maybe I'll see you around. Name's Adam."

She stood frozen, baffled. "Okay…"

The man held her gaze as he walked away. Mari pushed into the women's bathroom. She stood in front of the mirror getting a hold of herself, feeling terrorized and inebriated at once. *Who was that man? A molester? A murderer? Or maybe just someone a little… off.* She couldn't deny that his words had made her flustered. After all, she had never been called beautiful before. She stood with her hands on her hips, staring at her ghostly reflection. *So pale now. Pasty. But beautiful? No.* She pulled up her shirt to see her stomach in the mirror. *Thin? Maybe. Yes, that was good, could be thinner. But beautiful? No. No possible way.*

She dropped her shirt. The door burst open: not him. Just some old lady. Mari had thought for a moment it might be him. *Hoped?* But no, that was absurd. She pushed out of the bathroom door. There was music and a microphoned voice in the distance. The junior fashion show was getting back under way.

***

Ebony was up for her next epic pass on the runway. Grown men had stuck around, a little disgusted with themselves for sitting through the kiddie porn and bubblegum music that had preceded her, but it was worth it to get another glimpse of the dark-skinned Venus. Fortunately for them, she was wearing even less this time. Jamal stood on his tiptoes, blocking Mari's view of the spectacle. With each exaggerated step, Ebony's cleavage jiggled wildly; she was decked out in a low-cut top.

"Bounce, baby, bounce," called Jamal. Mari crossed her arms over the plateau of her chest, staring in awe at Ebony's fullness. The sense of inadequacy was nauseating. She turned around to put her eyes somewhere else.

Behind her, there were more people than she had remembered from the start—all there to watch Ebony, of course. One man was even standing on a bench, no doubt to catch a better view of the star. Yet the direction of his gaze, its steadiness, defied logic; he wasn't looking at the body on the runway. His eyes had been waiting for Mari to turn around. It was the man from outside the bathroom.

"Check that out," said Jamal as he poked Mari with his elbow. It was a redundant view of Ebony's ass.

"Yeah, okay," she said. Then she looked again behind her.

The man's face was still there, the same eyes awaiting hers. She held his gaze until the elbow stuck her again.

"*What?*" she said in annoyance.

"Who you lookin' at back there?" asked Jamal.

"No one," she lied. Jamal's eyes searched the crowd behind her. A new model made her way onto the runway. Mari saw the girl lose her footing and fall. It drew Jamal's attention back to the stage.

"Oh shit," he laughed as the girl scampered off. Mari looked back to where the man had been. He was no longer on the bench. Her eyes scanned the laughing faces of the crowd. The man was nowhere to be seen.

It was over, then. Whatever that had been. She felt relief and sadness that it was done. It was then a pair of hands came to rest on her waist. Jamal was in front of her; it couldn't have been him. The pair of hands had come from behind.

Her heart beat, beat harder, a beat surely heard by everyone there, but no, no one had heard, no one had seen the sight of them—she and this figure whose hands were laid upon her. Their spectacle had been eclipsed by the black goddess on the runway, wearing nothing this time, wearing less than nothing, less than the nothing she'd been born in, the nothing she would give birth in. And now this stranger's hands were on Mari, absurd hands, scraping at her, pulling her away, and she was going so easily, so easily and without a fight, receding into the crowd, watching the stage and the naked girl onstage recede as the man led her back—this man whose face she knew would be the one that had been missing when she had searched for it only moments ago.

She knew, and she let him lead her back, away from the nothing she would be losing, the nothing she would be leaving were she to leave this crowd, and this scene, and maybe even her own life, were this man to somehow take it away from her. But when he turned her around to look at her, to stand so close to her, she didn't see a madman in his eyes, not like the figure she had seen outside the bathroom, not like the maybe-molester or -monster, but a man who wanted her for something else, for something he had chosen her and only her for. *Her and only her*. Not the naked girl on stage, not the women in the audience with hatred in their eyes for the naked girl on stage, but her, the flawed one, the one who was nothing special. Her and only her, the meek.

Now *they* were the spectacle, the spectacle *for* the spectacle: for Ebony, who had spotted them from the end of the runway. She had stopped there in her dark brown bikini, a second skin that made her appear unclothed. She stood transfixed at the sight of her friend with the strange man. Jamal looked back to see where Ebony was looking. He saw Mari facing the man. They were close. Too close. His eyes caught the man's. The man was already glaring at him. Daring him to try and stop him. Jamal accepted the challenge, starting back into the crowd. He held the man's gaze until the man turned away, whispering something into Mari's ear. The whisper made her turn with him and break away from the back of the crowd. Jamal pushed hard against the people facing him, who were scattering now that Ebony had left the stage.

***

"Let's make like mall-walkers," said Adam to Mari. They walked briskly past the stores in the mall. "I think the guy you were with might be following us."

"That's just my friend's boyfriend," she said. "He can be a little protective sometimes."

"I don't blame him. Someone like you is worth protecting."

Her face reddened.

"You remember my name, right?"

"I think you said Adam."

"That's right. But you never told me yours."

"Mine's Mariana. Or Mari for short."

"Easy enough."

Jamal was behind them, keeping his distance. Adam could feel it.

"I could tell they trouble you, Mari," said Adam. "The crowd. That many people."

"Not them."

"What, then? *Her?* The one on stage?"

Mari nodded. *Had it been that obvious?*

"No matter. They should be watching *you* instead. Like I was."

He reached down and took her hand as they walked.

"You're shaking," he said. "Do I frighten you?"

"I'm not sure."

"Don't be afraid. I'll take you away from here."

"Where?"

"Somewhere we can be alone. Is that okay with you?"

"I'm not sure."

"That's okay. There's no pressure. For now, just follow my lead."

He led her through the food court area, then down the corridor to the bathrooms.

"Where are we going?" she asked.

"I thought maybe in here," he gestured toward the family bathroom. "Do you mind?"

Her stomach sank. "For what?"

Adam reconsidered: *too risky a place to carry it through.* "I have a bad bladder," he lied. "But I guess I can hold it. How about you, do you need to go before we leave?" he asked, planning anew.

"*Leave?*"

"If it's okay with you, I mean. Maybe I wasn't clear before. That's what I had meant."

"Oh…"

Adam's eyes moved aside, distracted. Footsteps were coming down the corridor. His eyes returned to hers. She suddenly looked pale enough to faint.

"You okay?" he asked.

"Just a little lightheaded."

He figured she was merely swooning with nerves, a virgin till now to any man's touch. Little did he know the truth of her condition: she had nearly starved herself to the brink of unconsciousness.

A man who wasn't Jamal rounded the corner, giving Adam and Mari a strange look before entering the men's bathroom.

"Maybe you should get some fresh air," Adam said to Mari. He walked her over to a door with a lighted *EXIT* sign above it and pushed it open, revealing a dumpster and the parking lot in twilight. He handed her a set of car keys. "Wait out here. I'll be right back."

"But…"

He let the door close in front of her as he remained in the building. New footsteps were coming down the corridor. He reached for the handle of the family bathroom. He entered and shut the door just as the footsteps he expected came to a halt outside the door. He banged on the inside of the door and shouted, "Mari's in here—she needs help!" A hand pushed the door open and in came Jamal. Adam grabbed him and locked his arm around his neck, pulling him down. He kept the hold locked with his other hand and clamped down with all his might as he was positioned under Jamal on the floor. Jamal kicked and struggled, but the grip was too strong to break. It only got tighter; tighter; until there was no more air, no more sound. Adam twisted Jamal's body to the floor, releasing him. He raised himself to his feet, looking down at the face of the man he had destroyed.

This was a marvel. He had taken a life—a life not his own to take. It was something he hadn't planned, and yet he had done it without hesitation. He was astounded by the strength and resolve he had exhibited.

He opened the door and left the bathroom. The corridor was empty. He walked over to the *EXIT* door and stepped outside. A wave of panic. She was gone.

"Down here," came a voice from below. It was Mari. She was slumped over, sitting with her back against the building. She looked pale and weak, her hands hanging over her knees.

"Are you alright?"

"Fine," she mumbled. "I guess you were right. I needed some fresh…" Her voice trailed off.

"Let's get you out of here." He held out his hand.

"Give me a minute. I can't see." She kept her eyes squinted, trying to find his arm. He reached down and pulled her up. "Oh jeez," she said, trying to get her footing. She stumbled momentarily.

"Just follow me." He kept his arm around her for support. "I'll take you to the car."

"But… but maybe I should tell…"

"Don't try to talk," he said. He took it as a blessing how weak she had become. An unquestionable sign—a sign he wouldn't dare question—as to how well things were falling into place.

He guided her through the parking lot. "Where did you put the keys?" he asked as they approached his car. Mari opened her mouth, but it wasn't language that came out—just a string of grunting sounds. Adam reached into her right jeans pocket and pulled out the keys. He unlocked the passenger door and eased her into the seat. As he shut the door, he heard the *EXIT* door of the mall burst open. A security guard came running out.

Adam walked calmly to the driver's side door. He opened it and dropped his weight into the seat and pulled the door shut. He started the car and backed out, turning in the direction opposite the mall. Looking in the rearview, he now saw two guards milling around instead of one. He pulled off at a normal speed, turning his lights on. He looked over at Mari, his prize: so pale in the night, glowing, like his headlights upon the roads that would lead them away from here to the refuge of his apartment, where they could finally be together, alone.

III. Bodies in the Dark

Mari awakened to a set of four walls. Each wall had a mouth and two eyes.

Wall one: "You know what he has done to you?"

Wall two: "Of course she knows."

Wall one: "You can't assume she knows."

Wall three: "Both of you shut up."

The walls began to close in. It wasn't a room anymore, it was a closet. She was sitting at the bottom of a small closet.

"Ask her where her clothes are," said a fourth wall—the one directly in front of Mari.

"You ask her," said wall three (to her right).

"I think she's noticed," said wall two (to her left).

"You can't assume that," said wall one (behind her).

Mari's knees were bent up in front of her. Thanks to the walls, she had noticed something troubling: she wasn't wearing any clothes.

"Pretty sure she's figured out what happened," said wall two.

"Maybe," said wall four. "But I'm the only one who could tell her for sure."

"I could tell her, too," said wall two.

"Yeah, but only based on what we could hear," said wall one.

"That's right," said wall four. "As the door, I was the only one who could actually *see* what happened in the room outside."

"What, you got eyes in the back of your head?" said wall three. "We all know you were closed the whole time. He only opened you and put her in here after he was done."

"As a matter of fact, I have two sets of eyes," said the door. "One in front, one in back. A handle, too. I'm special like that."

"Why not rub it in?" said wall three.

"Yeah," said wall two. "You should really watch your tone. Just because you're a door and we're the walls doesn't give you the right to belittle us."

"You're all just bitter," said the door.

Mari's hands reached up for the doorknob. She turned it and pushed with both hands.

"Ooh, that feels good," said the door. "I've never been turned from the inside."

"Get a hold of yourself," said wall three.

"Everyone quiet," said wall one. "We're all about to see what's out there."

"It's too dark," said wall two.

"Your eyes will adjust," said the door. "I'll see you guys later."

The door swung open. Mari peered into the dark of the room, her eyes wide open. Nothing. There was nothing to see. No shapes in the dark, no light to bathe the shapes. She looked back and forth across the abyss.

"That door must have some damn sharp eyes," said wall one. "Cuz I can't see a thing."

Kneeling, she plunged one foot, then the other, into the unknown. She listened. Nothing at first… then a drip. A drip that told her she was alive. Not dead. Not deaf. But alive. Alive, and maybe blind. Definitely violated—she knew that from the ache between her legs. But at least she had to be alive.

She moved toward the sound of the drip. It had given some dimension to the darkened space. Her hands fumbled along the wall and met a doorframe, then a doorknob. Cold air ran up her naked body from under the *had-to-be-a-front-door* as she turned its vertical lock horizontal. She twisted the handle, her eyes rejoicing at the sliver of dim nocturnal light seeping in: enough to prove she wasn't blind. Then the chain lock stopped the door cold.

Something creaked behind her. It was a swinging shape that creaked as it swung: a foot—*no, a naked leg*—dangling. An entire body was hovering in the dim light like magic. Then gravity broke the spell, bringing the body down along with the ceiling fan it had been hanging from. The sound startled Mari's hands away from the chain lock and she tripped, toppling a glass lamp that shattered under her leg. She reached in toward the light switch of the shattered lamp. Its click brought a flash that showed a face—a face that was moving toward her. Then the light bulb popped. She remembered the *had-to-be-a-bathroom* from which the dripping sound had emanated. It was bound to have a door that she could close on the face. The face, his crawling face.

She reached up for the bathroom door. The face had a hand that wrapped around her ankle. She turned the knob, leaning into the door and dropping. (*Dripping.*) Dropping away from the hand. (*Dripping.*) She could hear a dripping sink overhead. Below her, the tiles were cold and damp. She backed up against the wall as far as she could go.

There was light in here: a lit candle above the toilet. It shone enough light for her to see. Only, that was a curse now, not a blessing. She could only wait for the face to show. The face of her betrayer—of the predator who no longer deserved a name.

A set of fingers wrapped around the doorframe, pulling the top of the head into view. A forehead and nose, a mouth, a neck with a failed noose around it. Then his hand gripping a long and jagged sliver of glass from the shattered lamp. He stabbed it hard into his own throat and dragged it across. She finally met his eyes just as the light was leaving them.

"I'm sorry," he gurgled.

She let herself scream. His head collapsed into the blood pooling slowly across the bathroom floor.

Mari closed her eyes. The nightmare was over. She fell asleep to a dripping sound.

***

A dripping sound awakened her in the hospital. She opened her eyes to a brand new nightmare. An IV dripped food into her skeletal frame. They were feeding her without her permission. She tried to sit up.

"Mari?" came a voice from her bedside. A voice she knew as Ebony's. "Hold on, let me page the nurse."

"Wait," said Mari. "You've gotta help me. You've gotta help get this out of me." She gripped the IV that was part of her arm.

"Are you crazy?" said Ebony. *Crazy?* Mari heard the talking walls of Adam's closet, saw a flash of his dying face in her mind. Her ordeal came flooding back to her. But the IV was somehow more terrifying. She cursed herself for having let her body shut itself down in his bathroom, the same way it had shut itself down after getting into his car at the mall. In passing out, she had ceded control of her body: an unforgivable mistake.

"How long has this been in me?" she asked.

"Two days," said Ebony. "You've been in here two days... ever since they found you."

Mari became sickened with the thought of the two days' sustenance now in her system. She felt violated, and disgustingly fat. "They should have left me for dead," she said.

Ebony shuddered, taken aback. "*Dead?* You mean dead like Jamal?"

Mari let go of the IV. "*What?*"

"That monster took him," said Ebony. "That's what." Tears welled in her eyes. "So don't you be talking about wanting to be dead. You'd better praise God you're alive, no matter what kind of hell you've been through."

"Oh God, I'm so sorry for Jamal."

Ebony softened, taking Mari's hand in hers. She guided it up to her stomach. "He's still here," she said, pressing Mari's hand against the life Jamal had left behind. Mari smiled faintly, then suddenly looked aghast. She brought her hand up to her gaping mouth.

"What is it?" Ebony asked. But she had a feeling she knew what it was. Having assumed that Mari had been violated, she herself had been wondering the same thing.

"What if I'm...?" started Mari. "Do they know if I'm...?"

The nurse entered the room. Mari grabbed her by the arm as soon as she approached the bed. "Am I pregnant?" she asked, squeezing hard.

The nurse looked at Ebony. "Let's get the doctor in here," she said.

"Hold up," said Ebony. "Let me ask you something..." And she followed the nurse out of the room.

Mari turned her head toward the window. It looked out to the wall of the adjacent building, a barrier that blocked any view of the afternoon sky. The building's dirty red bricks were the color of blood. *His* blood. She remembered it spreading slowly across the bathroom floor. How it had reached her toes just before she lost consciousness. A dark pool beneath her legs, like a deathly menstruation.

It was a reminder.

She hadn't bled in months. In all these months upon the cross of her own making, her monthly cycle had shut itself down.

She couldn't be pregnant. Not when she no longer

menstruated. It was an unintended consequence of the hell she had put her body through.

Relief washed over her.

It left her free to turn her thoughts to the monster still inside her: the undying compulsion to deny herself food. She knew there was a name for what she was doing to herself, but she was too ashamed to let it pass through her lips. *His* name came easier—that other monster—whose seed her self-starvation had thwarted.

"Adam…" she whispered, her thoughts consumed with the violation of the IV, the fatness it was pumping into her, the deep down ugliness beneath it all that she knew even years of continued anorexia would never be able to starve out. She finished her sentence guiltily, as if finishing a meal: "did you really think that I was beautiful?"

Projectionist vs. Priest

It is a familiar scene. One I know by heart. So I sit back and wait for it to unfold. Wednesday afternoon again. The Temple is empty. As you enter for worship, you pause to remove your fedora, then solemnly make your way down the aisle. You sit without taking your trench coat off, in your usual row, your usual seat. You place your fedora over your lap, interlocking your fingers. Head bowed, you begin to pray.

The beam of my projector controls your prayers—the images to which you give your weekly praise. From up here in my seat in the projection booth, I can see you playing out your little ritual. Every Wednesday at the Temple Theater, a new feast for your eyes. A new sickness for your viewing pleasure. Today's malady features a well-hung priest and the nuns awaiting his confession on the other side of the gloryhole.

Whatever it takes to keep you coming back. To keep you coming by your own hand, alone. That, and that alone, keeps our agreement fulfilled. It's how I know you haven't returned to your old ways. I can see the proof with my very own eyes... which seem to be failing me at the moment. Because I could swear there's something off about the way your hands are moving. Something off about the way you're... well... *getting off.*

Make that something *way* off. Only one way to be sure.

Tap tap tap. Come on, turn around. Can't you hear me tapping on the glass? How about now? No soundtrack to drown me out.

Turn around already. Don't make me stop the movie. That does it. I'm flipping on the lights.

That gets Not You to finally turn around. I don't give him time to move after he sees me. I'm down the stairs in no time, pulling him back from the locked *EXIT* door. It's not like he's getting far with his pants around his ankles. I grab him by the lapels of his coat and slam his back against the wall.

"He sent you, didn't he?" I say. "To sit in his place."

"Man, I don't know what you're talking about."

"Where is he?!"

"Where is who?"

"The man who sent you here. What did he look like?"

"Look man, you've got the wrong—"

"How much did he pay you? I'll give you more." Before he can think, I hold up a fifty and slip it in his coat pocket. "Here's a little memory boost. Now tell me what he looked like while I'm still being *nice*." I hoist him up the wall for emphasis, his legs dangling.

"Okay, okay, man! I ain't tryna get hurt. Was an older guy with a beard. Kind of tall. Had a belly. I don't know the guy personally, okay? He just paid my way and gave me this shit to wear. I'm just here for a free nut, is that a crime?"

I let go of him, this man you sent. Because that's when it's sealed for me. You're doing it again after all these years. If you're not in here, that's what you're off doing. I know it by the logic of your rituals. Wednesday afternoon is the time you seek pleasure—it's when you'd steal your pleasures from *me*.

He pulls his pants up and scurries back to his seat. "Hang on," I say, getting an idea. If the next move is mine, I know how to play it. "Another fifty for the coat and hat."

If it's come to this, Father, then I'm coming to end it. Come Sunday, I will see you at Mass.

***

Sunday Mass. Where is your new favored child? I know he is in here somewhere, sitting amongst the believers, struggling with his faith now that it has been shaken, struggling with this thing that has happened to him. Wednesday, it must have been, that you took him into the back office—the back *orifice*, as I used to think of it—stealing away his religion. I know his troubled thoughts, since I was once in his shoes. With what he thought a haven now a hell, this temple—site of faith and sanctity—now insane, the very meanings of the rituals are changing for him. No longer is the water holy, no longer is it even water—it is your saliva, and when he dips his fingers in it, he is awash in your spittle again. And the kneeling and the bowing of the heads are empty, empty of their old meanings; they are now just reminders of your kneeling before him, and the bowing of his head afterwards in shame.

Let this new favored child lift his head from amongst the pews. I am here to end his shame. Let him raise his face so I can see that he has eyes. These others have holes where their eyes should be. They are blind to the things he and I have seen. He is the mini-Christ in the making; I, the Christ already made. Now comes you, our maker, emerging in your vestments to address the congregation that hangs on your every word:

"The ultimate sacrifice is the sacrifice of a child. Abraham knew this well."

Confess.

"One day, out of nowhere, God asked Abraham to perform the impossible. He said to Abraham, 'Take your son Isaac, your only one, whom you love, and offer him up as a sacrifice on a height that I will point out to you.' Now imagine you are Abraham. Imagine what you have to lose. Future generations have been promised to you through Isaac. He is your future; he is also just a child."

Like the child in here you are surely violating.

"And you are to raise your knife to him—raise your knife to this innocent child. Could you do it?"

You did.

"Do this for me: imagine leaving, as Abraham did, early in the morning, setting out with Isaac to the place of sacrifice. As you near the site, knowing what you will do there, knowing what you will do to the child, this child, this naively innocent child, says to you, 'Father, here are the fire and the wood, but where is the lamb for the sacrifice?' And as tears well in your eyes, you must lie to him, you must force yourself to reply, 'God himself will provide the lamb for the sacrifice.' For it is impossible to tell the child that *he* is the lamb; that *he* is to be the object of sacrifice."

The object of your gratification.

"So you continue to the place where you are to build the altar, and you do, you build it, and you lay the wood down, and you bind the child's arms, the arms of this naively innocent child, and perhaps he is crying now, and perhaps you are, too. Crying in your guilt, in the knowledge that what you are doing is wrong. And though you know it to be wrong, this thing you are doing, and cannot forgive yourself while you are doing it, you have faith that God will forgive you afterward—that He wouldn't have you doing this for no reason."

No reasons beyond your own.

"So you lay down the child on the altar, on top of the wood, and you prepare yourself, prepare your knife to bring it down on him. And as your knife is raised in your hand, you see the terror and confusion in the eyes of the child, a child that has trusted you, a child you have loved…"

A child who has loved you back.

"A voice tries to stop you, a voice that is the child's but not the child's, crying, 'Do not lay your hand on the boy or do the least thing to him.' The voice might be God's voice, but you do not hear it. You have already crossed the line."

How many more times, Father?

"Of course, Abraham was able to restrain himself—not that that was the point of God's test. The point was how far he was willing to go. How much he was willing to do in God's name. Let us pray."

Look at me. That's right. Like the outfit?

"I confess to almighty God, and to you, my brothers and sisters, that I have sinned through my own fault, in my thoughts and in my words, in what I have done, and in what I have failed to do. And I ask blessed Mary, ever-Virgin, all the angels and saints, and you, my brothers and sisters, to pray for me to the Lord, our God. May almighty God have mercy on us, forgive us our sins, and bring us to everlasting life. Amen."

Next, I'm behind a boy in the Communion line as you offer him the sacramental bread.

"The body of Christ," you say.

The boy looks up and takes the offering: "Amen." And he consumes the host. I watch your eyes follow him a few seconds too long as he walks away.

When your eyes return, it is me standing before you. I do not open my mouth to receive the offering. I simply glare at you with supreme indignance.

"I've been expecting you," you say. "Why not take that ridiculous hat and coat off and stay a while?"

"I'll see you Wednesday afternoon," I say. "Or I break the agreement. Meaning you can kiss your good name goodbye."

***

Wednesday afternoon. Back in the projection booth at the start of the show. Praying that you will be down there when I open my eyes. When I do, I can't believe what I see. You or not you with a smaller you beside you, his head rising just above the seat.

You. Sick. Son of a bitch.

Finger stops the projector. Feet run down the stairs. Hands grab you and pull you up from your seat. You are not you. I look to the child. The child has a grown-up face.

"Where is he?" I ask your stand-in—a different hired doppelganger than last week. This time, he has a midget sitting beside him. A midget to make me think it is a child.

"He's waiting for you at the church," says the man in my grasp.

"Bring the movie back," the midget says.

Run to the church, then through it, to the back. Here through the office door is where it happened every Wednesday afternoon, and where it will surely be happening now. Only this time, I am here to stop it in the way no one could for me.

Lights flash beneath the threshold. I listen for screaming. Give me strength as I open this door.

The door creaks open. There is a loud rattling sound. There are lights flashing brightly onto a screen. I trace them back from the screen to the projector—it is rattling from a corner of the room. All is dark, save the screen. That is where I find the boy. In the image, he is bound facedown to the altar. You stand behind him, your member in your hand, preparing it to enter him from behind.

Your face is younger. The boy is no one I recognize from Sunday.

There in the corner, I see your older face. You watch

me as I watch the screen. Your older face is in the darkened part of the room. You are huddled in a corner there. In darkness. There is no new favored boy with you. The only favored boy is on the screen. He is the only boy in the room out of the four of us. There is the you in the corner and your double on the screen. There is me and then the boy I was long ago.

That time you recorded us: I had let it slip my mind. Now my knees buckle at the reminder. A first wave of nausea, like an old, familiar weakness. Then anger, terrible anger, all the anger I thought I'd left behind. The anger of a child who grew up believing you could be saved. Even if it meant forsaking any kind of respectable life to watch over you. Whatever it took to keep the ritual protected. To keep any others like me protected. Until you went and defied it. De*filed* it. Our ritual. As if our agreement was some kind of joke. But as you can see, no one in the room is laughing. And one of us is finally taking up the sword.

The knife. Lying at your feet. Positioned there. By you. As more than just a strong suggestion. As a *supplication*. The final request of a sinner on his knees. And who am I to deny you? It's not like I ever have before.

"Do it," you say.

"Shut your mouth." My hand shuts it *for* you, muffling your poisonous snout. The knife has made its way into my other hand. I hold its tip beneath your chin, pushing it up into the soft skin under your beard.

"Is this how you want it? Huh?"

Your eyes shut tightly. The skin of your throat starts to cave beneath the pressure of the knife.

"Shhhh. There's nothing to be afraid of. It's just between you and me."

A spot of blood forms under the tip.

"It occurs to me... I don't deserve this life you gave

me." I twist the handle, rotating it slowly right, then left. "Do you not agree?"

Your pitiful whimper vibrates against my hand.

"I mean, seriously. Watching over you all these years? And now *I've* gotta be the one to do this?"

I push up harder, sinking the tip in deeper as I turn the handle right, then left. Right, then left. Your whimper becomes a full-blown wail.

"Open your eyes," I say. They stay closed. "Open them!"

You do; tears are streaming down your face. A thin line of blood trails down your neck. I toss away the knife and shove your mouth, toppling you over.

"It won't be me."

I rise to my feet.

"You wanna die? You do it by your own goddamn hand, just like the rest of us."

The screen has gone blank. I follow the beam of the projector to the machine and click it off.

"Show's over." The room goes dark. "I'll see you Wednesday afternoon. Or by God, I swear to you…" I take the reel out of the projector. "Your beloved congregation will be seeing this little classic on the news."

"Go to hell," you mutter from the dark.

To which I respond: "I live there."

There is light through the threshold. I cross it with the reel—the weight of its leverage, the renewal it all but ensures. The ritual will resume. It will endure. It is the only true religion I have ever known.

Yellow Light, Red Light

I only had an instant to either stop or keep going, and in that instant, I let momentum decide. I crossed the line just as the yellow light turned red. Next thing I knew, there were blue lights flashing in my rearview.

I hadn't been speeding before the stoplight. I hadn't robbed a bank or committed any major crime. I had merely been on my way to work and hit a yellow light, forcing a split-second decision to either slam the brakes or continue through the intersection. A relatable scenario if there ever was one. A forgivable occurrence if I had in fact done anything wrong.

But none of this matters to the officer who has pulled me over. I can tell from his stern demeanor he's not interested in any explanations or excuses. I have none to offer him anyway. I refuse to request understanding where none is being willingly volunteered. I simply await the outcome of the traffic stop, which he hands me through the window after running my license and registration. It's not a warning. It's a ticket. A yellow carbon copy that reads *RED LIGHT VIOLATION* in stark black print.

But isn't this the way it always is, on the receiving end of a blind man with power. The man with the power always seems to be blind, as if the power itself has shorted out his eyes. Eyes that dare not grant me the privilege of being *seen*. Who am I to him, anyway, but another fish on his hook? And what is this to me? Nothing new. Matter of fact, it happens all the time: someone like me, who goes out of his way to imagine himself in the shoes of others, left at the mercy of an authority figure who won't imagine himself in mine—with only the power he holds standing between us.

Pity the man with empathy, for he is weak. The

power never seems to be in his hands.

Least of all now, as I sit here beneath the judgment of this figurehead of all that I have thought wrong with the world since as far back as I can remember. The staggering amount of authority placed into the hands of the far too merciless and unkind. And as his baby blue eyes reflect back their black and white conception of what I have done and who I am and what I am capable of, I am convinced, they do not know. *They do not know.* How little they know of the anger within me, and the wildness of my scattering thoughts.

Thoughts that overtake me once I have taken the ticket, their green light the yellow sheet between my hands.

I imagine Mr. Policeman has a quaint little home in the suburbs. He has a wife who is pregnant with a junior Mr. Policeman, a child who will grow up to be like his father someday. When Mr. Policeman comes home, his wife (along with the junior policeman in her belly) greets him at the door, asking how his day of protecting and serving went. And he invariably tells her he is all protected- and served-out. He steps inside his home and it becomes *his* turn to be served in exchange for the protection he offers his wife.

She loves his baby blue eyes and the feeling of being safeguarded by a man who enforces the law. She knows he would never allow anyone to hurt her or the junior policeman in her belly, and that anyone who tried would pay dearly for it. She fears for her husband's life sometimes, but knows that's only natural given the dangers that come with his line of work. She has faith that God will keep him safe and bless their lives in return for his daily sacrifice.

There is much for Mr. Policeman to be thankful for. His home. His wife. The baby on the way. The courage to put on the badge every morning.

　　　　　　　　　　　　NATHANIEL BLACKHELM

But then there are the nights. Those cursed nights when his wife beats him in the race to sleep, and in the first moments of her slumber, the lie also sleeps. The lie that he has any means of protecting his family from harm. And as he starts to listen for noises outside their window and the quietest of footsteps up the stairs to their room, his imagination darkens, dreaming the deadliest of fates for his wife and unborn child. He begins to wish his wife would awaken, bringing the lie back from the shelter of her dreams. But then she might sense the nearness of the pistol in the hand he has draped around her belly. If he can keep her from detecting it, he can have his two tranquilities at once: both the security of his firearm and the soothing warmth of the life within her womb.

Sleep comes, if he is lucky. At some point, he has to stop listening for the footsteps. He has to start believing they won't come. There is life kicking against his hand—perhaps against the gun he is clenching. He reads it as a message from the unborn, reminding him there is no good reason to be so afraid. The danger, like the fear, is surely all in his head.

And then it is morning, and as his wife shifts awake, he finds himself scrambling to hide the gun, realizing, *This is the way I fell asleep last night.*

My thoughts, I fear them steering towards something sinister. Yet here is my chance to take the wheel... turning them... trying to determine their course... imagining... it catches up to him sometimes. The pettiness of what he does every day. It has to. He has to know. At some point, it has to come back and hit him hard. Maybe it's in the afternoon, when the morning's fishing is done, and he sits in his squad car remembering the real fish he used to catch with his father. How they would go out in the rowboat with their lines in the water and he would boast to his father of the criminals he would catch someday. Even that far back, he knew a day would come when he would step into his father's shoes, serving greatness in the name of the law.

But when he grew up and joined the force, a different reality emerged. A different set of truths than the ones he had grown up with. Things came out about his father. Disheartening things. Detailed accounts from the mouths of the elders who had served with the man and knew his exploits firsthand. The Rip Van Winkles he would pull in his squad car, sleeping through hours of radio calls. The empty mini bottles clinking around his floorboard even as he would be tailing one of the subjects of his countless DUI traffic stops. He would toss a few back in the driver's seat of the cruiser as he awaited the right target to emerge from one of the local drinking holes at closing time. A few miles down the road, he would pull them over and arrest them for being over the limit. His favorites were the businessmen with clean records who were visiting from out of town. They were usually the ones who pleaded and wept. He loved showing them how fragile their carefully built white-collar, college-educated careers were. How a single mugshot and misdemeanor charge could do worlds of damage to the reputations of big shots like them. It made him feel, even briefly, like the bigger man—an even better buzz than the alcohol in his bloodstream.

And then there was his little side hobby: the working girls he would frequent for sexual favors at the end of his shifts. In exchange for not taking them in on prostitution charges, all he asked was that they take *him* in with the law enforcement discount applied. It was a much more thrilling perk than the occasional free meal he'd receive from the local dining establishments.

These and other anecdotes, the elders of the force

gleefully recounted as they were on their way out, retiring, just as Mr. Policeman was beginning his law enforcement career. He was entering the revolving door of the police station as they were exiting a final time, the door spinning round and round. Their yarns of his father's transgressions, spinning into the ears of the new rank and file—Mr. Policeman's fellow rookies. Those who were the sons of the elders already knew the stories. They'd heard them growing up. They even knew the truth behind his father's medical retirement—the career-ending knee injury he had suffered in the line of duty. The fact that what had been reported as a random assault was in fact an act of retaliation: a vindictive pimp had taken a crowbar to Mr. Policeman's father's knee for having bullied his top earner into unprotected, uncompensated sex. It was the reason he walked with a limp in his later years.

Speaking of limps, Mr. Policeman was now staggering as he exited that fateful revolving door, whereas entering, he had been walking tall and proud. Within months, his fellow rookies would come to surpass him in the field— a prophecy easily fulfilled, given his father's crippling legacy. What more could you expect, when Mr. Policeman was made of the same compromised DNA?

And now, here he was, that officer grown older, fishing at his favorite intersection, the one with the shortest yellow light, casting his line into the traffic, hoping against hope for greatness, for the biggest possible catch.

Son of a bitch hook hurts like crazy, sunken in as it is through my cheek. He's got me, already had me, but he still won't let go, maybe trying to pull off the side of my face. The ticket is beside me and he's back in his cruiser, but his hook is still caught in my mouth. He didn't bother removing it before he left my window. He didn't even ease the sting. A little humanity would have served that purpose, but there is none to be had from this man. I am convinced now. Before, no, because I had imagined that maybe there were reasons for his actions, things in his life that could explain his choice in penalizing me for something so small and understandable. Now though, no way. I've changed my mind. How stupid of me to have given this stubborn petty cruel man the benefit of the doubt. This cold as ice heartless waste of skin and air with a badge. Because in a hundred years, done a hundred times over, he would never return the favor for me. He would never put himself in my shoes.

Reverse the roles, and I would at least let this end. Not him, though. He has instructed me that I am free to go, yet has left me with this sting still in my system, this barbed hook still in my cheek, its line running ruthlessly from his window. I can see it; him; and my impotence, in the rearview. Here I am, a decent, unassuming man who would have already been at work had I not been pulled over to be judged and belittled for what amounts to a cosmic nothing. Ridiculous. People do this to each other: they ruin each other's lives over the smallest things. Entire lives wasted, wasting others' time. Unbelievable that they get away with it. They keep doing it, and they keep getting away. There is always something there for them to hide behind: a badge, a gavel, a title, a last name—always something that keeps them protected from reprisals. Invincible, like this one, who steals my time—time here and to be spent thinking back on this humiliation, hours, days, maybe even years from now. And the point... the only point to it all is the one sticking through my mouth, stretching the skin up toward the window as I pull off to drive away. A hook still on a line that I now drive against, still in the hands of the man with no sympathy I drive away from, who holds me having released me, by this hook

NATHANIEL BLACKHELM

pulling off my face.

So long then, face. I doubt I will miss you, given the impotence you remind me of. I can imagine a no more fitting way to replace you than to press the gas like so and let this son of a bitch hook have its way, set as it seems on pulling harder the farther we get—though I no longer believe we'll be leaving. No, Mr. Policeman has left too great an impression for that now that his hook has left you smeared across the window. He has invited our return, having refused to cut his line—or even to just originally let us go. So we return, then. One by one. You first, as I roll down the window, freeing the hook and *youmyface* that it holds. When you reach him, which soon you will, give him a smile and send this message: the rest of me is not far behind.

I will simply need a moment to freshen up. Gather my thoughts. Clear my mind, so close now to the elements. So near to spilling out, without the skin. All preparations for a decision I have to make as to how far I'm willing to go.

A stoplight in the distance turns from green to yellow. I only have an instant to decide. To let the momentum decide *for* me. The momentum that has *become* me. So much easier it is as Momentum Incarnate, with the decision already made in My name.

Back in the boat with his father now, Mr. Policeman sits with his line in the water, waiting, and following his father's lead. He looks at this man beside him, this man he's been doubting ever since the revolving door, and he begins to doubt all that was ever certain about him—his goodness, his purpose, even the way he catches fish. The two men don't talk or trade glances, only stare at their lines cutting into the water. Below is the unknown, complete with moving shapes and mysterious forces, some dangerous, some benign, but all potential threats to the calm of the surface amidst the awkward new silence between father and son. One thing is certain: they are no longer safe here. This is no longer a familiar place. It seems alien, like each man to the other—strangers, once kindred, now drifting irreparably apart.

His father farther than ever now, Mr. Policeman wills himself back to the moment before the revolving door, to the instant before entering it, so he can put a stop to the elders this time. A *permanent* stop. Because they deserved nothing less for their absence of mercy, for their knowing dissemination of the stories that had ruined everything he believed in—everything that had made him want to follow in his father's footsteps since the time he was a child.

But as he draws his newly issued service weapon and pulls the trigger at the first hint of a word from their venomous mouths, he hears, instead of a gunshot, the sound of a violent splash behind him and finds himself back in the boat, snapped out of his vengeful reverie by the sight of his father sinking hard and fast into the deep. Then a tremendous pull on the fishing line, and Mr. Policeman steadies his grip, hoping it is his father trying to pull himself back, back up, back up into the light of good favor, the good favor and adoration of his son, this grown man who now pulls so desperately against the line, trying to steady it against the ungodly forces of life's disappointments, against the hopelessly earthbound flow of passing traffic at the shortest of yellow lights where every fish he baits is the same and none of them is ever a big catch… until Me. The One that returned. The One that from the depths of the unknown beneath the boat pulled his father down and took him only seconds ago, now pulling Mr. Policeman in by the line he keeps extended into traffic at all times, refusing to let go.

Let go. Just let go. If only he would have just let it go. But he wouldn't, and still won't, and wouldn't given the chance again, so here we are descending past the unknown to the depths of the unimaginable, where I have not even imagined going before.

My darkest hour. His bedroom at night. Lying next to his sleeping wife.

As him.

I have never tried taking empathy this far—to the point of inhabitation. Not just putting myself in another's shoes, but actually wearing their flesh and bone.

The fit of Mr. Policeman's couldn't be better—or more fitting as a means to an end.

His family's.

Green light, and I am gone, off to gathering his comforts.

Drawing one from the bedside drawer. His gun.

Drawing nearer the source of the other—his wife— whose back obscures the warmth I seek.

The light still green.

Draping my arm around her belly.

Still green.

Hovering the gun over her skin.

Still green.

Pressing the barrel against her womb, against the warmer-than-I-had-imagined.

Please, yellow.

Pushing me farther, making me push the barrel hard.

Please, yellow.

The green triggering my finger.

But still green.

The color signaling a decision already made.

Not now, yellow.

I can't stop the momentum.

Too late, yellow.

No stopping me now.

Not even with the life inside of here kicking back against this cold steel in my hand the prayer for mercy that screams, *These eyes, they want to see! These eyes, they want to see!* nor even with this scream in his mother's eyes as her husband's fingers (that are mine) pry them open to meet his baby blue eyes (that are mine) as they plummet her gaze toward certain atrocity, the sight matching the sensation of the gun pressed mercilessly against their (our?!) kicking pleading coward of an unborn son whose prayer for mercy continues to scream…

These eyes, they want to see! These eyes, they want to see!

Even that does not stop me. For all I can think with my finger against this trigger is the way we are all destined to be blind.

Red light now, as my imagination slams the brakes, bringing the thoughts to a screeching halt. Instead of a gun in my hand, there is only this yellow sheet of paper, where Mr. Policeman's charge reads the same as before. He gave me this ticket for running the red light—but what for crossing the line?

Humiliating sirens still flashing in my rearview. He is waiting for me to pull away. First I'll need a moment to gather my thoughts. I would hope that isn't too much to ask.

The Darkness in the Room is Me

So tell me, sleeping beauty…

What type of bedtime story would you like to hear?

I will tell you one in whispers while you sleep.

The one I have in mind, you may have heard before—in one form or another—but you've never heard it told like this.

Never so you couldn't help but listen.

Never so you believed it could be real.

Although this one isn't make believe, like the one you may have been expecting. It isn't a fairytale, where the prince is always faithful to his princess… even after they've been married a number of years.

This isn't one of those stories. This isn't anything like a storybook, where you wish it would happen to you. Where you awaken wanting to go back to the dream.

This isn't a dream you can awaken from. This is the voice that has become your sleep. The whisper that can end your dreams as it begins them…

With a fairytale's opening phrase.

Once upon a time…

There was a faithful wife who thought she had a faithful husband. She radiated faithfulness, even in her sleep. His unfaithful thoughts kept him awake at night. But they were only thoughts. He had never acted on them. To him, that made him worthy of her love. That at least distinguished him from the husbands who cheated on their wives. Even if he was no different in the dirty little workings of his mind.

But people were allowed to think. That's why our thoughts were made to be private. There was no reason for his wife to know. Not when she had always considered him to be different from other men. More trustworthy. Less likely to stray. Purer of heart. At least that's what she believed. That's why she had chosen him in the first place. He didn't think that nobly of himself, but why shouldn't she go on believing it? After all, he had never acted on his secret thoughts, so maybe it was technically true.

For a long time, he tried to be good. He tried his best. But there was just so much beauty around him on a daily basis. So much delectable flesh, with so many orifices to imagine filling. And at the center of everything was the gaping hole he had inside himself that no amount of love and affection from his home life could seem to fill. So mentally, he sought refuge in imagined rendezvous with other partners. Many other partners.

Porn helped sometimes, but the women were just pixels on a screen. You couldn't touch them. It was inherently limited. He increasingly longed for something real. A real and tactile extramarital experience, or even *series* of experiences. Because thoughts and fantasies just weren't cutting it anymore. That was clear to him. He had been good for so long that at this point, he was failing his true self. The thoughts and fantasies deserved better. They deserved a chance behind the wheel. To not just think for him, but to act on his behalf. At least for a little while. Because that's the only way he could think of to rid himself of the urges. The only way he could think of to get them out.

I told him he'd done a good job of describing his dilemma to me… and why couldn't he just explain it to his wife the same way?

"Are you kidding?" he laughed. "It doesn't work that way. I say that to her, and I not only hurt her deeply… I ruin the possibility of ever getting away with anything. Why raise her suspicions, if I can find another way of doing it without her ever having to know?"

"Well, John… it *is* John, right?"

"John, yeah. We'll go with that."

"Well, John, what I was gonna say is, it sounds like you've thought this over quite a bit."

He nodded.

"I see. So let me get this straight. You want a taste of something filthy so you can get yourself clean."

Another nod.

"I believe that can be arranged."

Welcome to the next part of the story, snorey.

Welcome to his little window to the world. The indoor food court lined with floor-to-ceiling windows where he sat during his lunch breaks, watching the shapes pass by outside.

No food on his plate, though he was hungry.

No shape not devoured with his eyes.

His all you can eat buffet of the flesh… where he never failed to fill himself up.

To feel up as many women as he possibly could.

To fuck more women than you could count.

It was more than even I could count, watching him as he projected his thoughts through the glass. He would stop them in their tracks, bending them over backwards, or making them go down on their knees. His tongue, his hands, his member all over them… the countless women who passed by outside.

Some had husbands… he fucked them while they were watching.

Some had children… he fucked them over their cries.

He fucked them in front of whoever was with

them… if he didn't fuck that person too.

I watched him fuck them all.

The whole world—through the window—with only his eyes…

That were my windows into his needs.

I read him like a book from the other side of the window. Then I came in and walked up to where he sat.

"Enjoying the view?" I said. We started talking like old friends. Turns out we had a mutual interest in the nuances of the female form.

Across the table, he began confessing to me what he couldn't to his wife.

And our first business lunch was underway.

His confessions spilled over into our next lunch meeting.

He told me things you wouldn't believe.

He said there were pieces of her all over the place in the dark somewhere. He had her scattered all over, assembling her from the pieces of the bodies he had been collecting. The bodies he had been hiding away. He told me about the parts he had severed and paired, the most remarkable of their shape and kind.

That pair of lips, with this pair of eyes.

That ass, with this pair of tits.

Or maybe this pair.

Or maybe…

The way he told it, he might not have even found the right pair yet. It might have still been out there, waiting to be severed from the woman of which it was a part.

He told me no woman's parts were safe from him.

No matter how young. No matter how married.

Any woman in sight was fair game.

No body was spared from the scrutiny of his glances. From the threat of being taken apart. Private part from private part, limb from limb. To be made a part of *her*.

He said he didn't know how she would look once the parts were assembled. All he could do was spread out the pieces for me, to show me how she was coming along.

And this is what he had so far.

An imperfect human collage. A bundle of mismatched parts. Nothing close, we agreed, to the masterpiece that would justify the risk. That would justify him cheating on his wife.

"I want her to be just right," he told me. "If I am to do this thing."

"Then keep painting me the picture, so I can make sure I have the right girl for you."

And as he described for me a collage of the best parts he had severed into the dark space of his memory from the bodies of the women he had seen in public while next to his wife and at work while away from his wife and through the window to the world we sat behind, it occurred to me, as it always does on such occasions:

I have just the right person in mind.

He started our next meeting heavy with doubt. "I don't know if I can do this," he said.

I asked him to tell me what was wrong.

"It's not right," he said.

"You mean, to do this to your wife?"

He nodded.

"Because she is faithful to you?"

Another nod.

"Well, do you think she could ever understand what you're going through?"

"I don't know. Even I don't understand it. I should be happy with the things I have."

"And you are," I said. "But you still want more."

"Yeah. But I shouldn't."

"There's nothing wrong with wanting more, John. I wanted more once. I wanted more when there was no one like me around to help me get it. And you know what happened? I lost everything because of it. Because I was careless in the arrangements I made."

I steeled myself before opening up to the man.

"Believe it or not, I used to have a wife like you do," I said. "She was faithful to me just like yours. She did everything for me. She was beautiful. And yet I wanted more. I wanted to tell her… but she ended up *seeing* it instead. You know the story… how the wife walks in on her husband… well, that happened because I was sloppy… and then I lost it all. She ended up disappearing on me. Because I didn't have someone like me to help me out. But you *do*. That's why I'm here for you. To arrange this thing for you the right way. You don't have to be careless like I was. It's all in the way you arrange things. That's what I do for people. For men like you. I arrange things so they can get what they want."

I could still see a measure of doubt in his eyes. "If she ever found out…"

"She won't," I said. "Not unless you tell her. Or you're stupid enough to leave pictures behind. Which reminds me…"

I reached into my pocket. "You remember that picture you described for me last week?"

He nodded.

"Do you want to see how it turned out?"

Another nod. I laid the Polaroid down in front of him.

"She's the closest I have to what you described."

He stared in awe at the naked body in the photo.

"Holy…" He took the picture in his hand, shaking his head in disbelief. "What's her name?"

"She goes by Camille."

"Camille," he repeated.

"You see, John, this is what I do for a living. I take what's in *there*," I said, touching my finger to his forehead. His eyes raised up. "And bring it out into the living world for you and only you to taste."

He recoiled, brushing his forehead where my finger had just made contact. He flipped the photo over, staring carefully into my eyes. "You're not fucking with me here, are you?"

I leaned back in my seat. Taking my time before I answered. Giving him my most reassuring look. "I'm in the fuck business, John. I'm not here to fuck you over."

He stared all the way through me until he was satisfied—until a calm had washed over his face. Then he turned the photo back over and resumed his previous staring match with the body.

"First I want to meet her," he said.

I arranged for her to pass by the window to the world in the midst of our final arrangements. He was getting down to business as we awaited her arrival.

"We can do the payment thing once I've met her," he said. "Now what about a time and place for the private meetup between just me and her?"

"Any time but daytime. And any place you choose is fine."

"Why not daytime? This is the best time for me."

"Because she has school, John."

"Oh," he said, taken aback. "You mean like college?"

"She's legal, if that's what you're worried about."

"Oh." His face relaxed. "But how is she able to come today, then?"

"She has a small break between classes."

"I see." He hesitated. "You sure when the time

comes, it has to be at night? I mean, what about late afternoon?"

"Sorry, John. Only nights for her."

"Okay," he said, thinking to himself.

"Worried about your home schedule?"

"Yeah. Me and the wife spend all our nights together."

"You don't have any friends you go out with?"

"Not really. It's just me and her."

"That's right. You did describe things as rather... *claustrophobic*. Well, could you think up an excuse to get out of the house for one night of your life?"

He shook his head. "She knows me too well. We know each other's routines."

"I see. Then I can only think of one other way. But I don't know..."

"What is it?"

"You might think it's too extreme." I was about to go out on a little limb.

"Just tell me," he said. As if his mind was already going there.

"It's a sedative. Something that will put her to sleep for a little while."

And the limb... hadn't broken. It was now supporting both of our weight. His face was calm and inquisitive.

"For how long?" he asked.

"Long enough to get this out of your system."

"What is it, like a roofie or something?"

"Similar. You dissolve it in her drink at bedtime. Real simple to use. And totally safe, in case you're wondering."

"How do I get it? From you?"

I shook my head. "It's not something I usually carry around."

"That's a shame. I wanted this thing to happen this

week…"

"So do I. Which is why—"

Just then, a tap on the window. He turned his head to look. The look on his face said it all.

"—I had *her* bring it."

And there she was, in all her glory: the girl from the photo, in the flesh. Albeit fully clothed, in jeans and an *X-Men* t-shirt.

"I believe you have a visitor," I said.

She stared at him through the glass.

"This is Camille," I said. "Let's finish our arrangements so you can meet."

He couldn't peel his eyes away.

"John," I said.

She was grinning devilishly at him.

"John," I repeated. "You're not my only meeting today. The envelope I asked you to bring?"

He reached into his pocket and blindly withdrew an envelope.

"Here," he said. He handed it to me distractedly.

"Well, what are you waiting for?" I said. "Go introduce yourself."

But as he rose from his chair, she started to leave.

"Where is she going?"

"She's a busy girl, John. Better catch her while you can. Only she knows the time and place."

"But I thought you said that would be up to—"

"You'd better hurry if you're gonna catch her."

His eyes left mine. She was no longer outside the window. He rose and hurried toward the exit.

"Nice doing business with you," I said, feeling the dull weight of the envelope full of hundred-dollar bills.

This is the part where you should definitely keep your eyes

closed.

The part where he threw his life away.

This was not a projection of himself he was sending through the window.

These were not his thoughts from behind the glass.

The glass was behind him now.

It was in front of me.

I was looking at him through his window to the world.

Watching him catch up to her.

Seeing her turn around.

His hand on her arm.

Their embrace.

The way his mouth lingered next to her neck.

Nostrils flaring. Scent inhaling.

Eyes closed.

Tight hug.

Time out.

This was real. This was him. Everything from his hands, to her everything within his hands… to her fingers, leaving something in his pocket. An envelope with the sedative wrapped in a folded note. Its written message giving notice of their time and place, that I had decided…

And by extension, also yours and mine.

Because you are sleeping, I assume you drank the sedative.

Because you are alone, I assume he is with her.

Everything goes according to plan, then.

Everything goes as arranged.

Oh, my dear, sleeping beauty: it appears you've been left in the dark.

He likes doing that to you. He even turned the lights out behind him as he left you in the room tonight. But I turned them back on as I came in. I thought you wouldn't mind. The light certainly doesn't mind you.

It paints you favorably, just as I had in my rendition of you based on your husband's scattered descriptions. I had to sort through his confessions for only what pertained to *you* in order to assemble a perfect collage of my own. One that matched the memory of the divine wife I once had, who, like yourself, radiated faithfulness even in her sleep. How long I have waited for someone clean enough to make *me* so clean as to be worthy of her again. Someone like you, inside of whom I can finally return to her grace.

I am coming home to her now. I don't want to come quickly. Because it all has to come out first. All the sins, released. All the stains from the arrangements I have made, made clean... before I leave from inside of you tonight.

Hear my confession. Better yet... *feel* it.

My original sin... the one between myself and my daughter. As if the body she grew into wasn't tempting enough, we came to find out that she could change it. Remold and rearrange it into whatever fleshly shape she pleased. The possibilities were endless, limited only by imagination. And like any man, I wanted to try them all. Every shape and size, every texture and color of the female form. You name it, you *describe* it, and she could make her body mimic it for a limited time. Any variation or deviation, any combination of proportions... any and every woman's body made possible. Made accessible. Even those too cartoonishly proportioned to naturally exist. Imagine that gift—that curse, some would say—passed down the family line... my side of the family, of course, where everything is dark and filthy... and where we are all uniquely gifted, no two gifts ever being the same. And now imagine the complement of her ability existing in my own: for while she can change herself physically into the fantasy of any man, I can read any man's fantasy from his most intimate thoughts.

Put us together, and you have our seedy existence… selling her malleable body to johns like your husband, who lie to their wives about their whereabouts just as they lie to me about their real names. Well, now comes the part when I tell you where your dear husband Henry is tonight.

The two of them are together, in the dim light of her high school bathroom. And as he tastes the flesh for which he unknowingly traded yours, he is tasting my original sin. Every part of it. Every part of the body she grew into that I tainted, that was and still remains every part my own flesh and blood. She was born with her mother's sanctity and I ruined it… then sold what remained into the world to prove I wasn't the only one who was fallible. That I wasn't the only one who would sacrifice his life for the flesh we are delivered into, but never from… the covers that in hiding our insides will always mislead us, leading us into temptation for the rest of our lives… leading those like your husband to trade the pure for the filthy… divinity, for the raw human form… as he has in leaving you alone tonight in exchange for a rented set of orifices and an hour of rented time.

But being led into the arms of a body stitched together from parts severed from memory and held together by lust, one can only wait for regret to tear it apart. And in the moment one comes, one feels the masterpiece breaking down… piece by threaded-together piece. The body before him is the same, but he has lost his appetite for it… her flesh, the same set of entrées he has been greedily devouring, but he has already had more than his fill… enough to make him want to throw up. And as he cleans up—though he won't ever be able to get clean—he realizes what he has left at home.

The only true masterpiece. The one that is forever… unless she were to find him out.

The *real* him.

The parts of him she still didn't—

No...

Don't want to come yet. Don't ever want to come. But I've stayed too long inside of you. Look at what you've done to me. I've lost track of time... you've rearranged the arranger himself.

I'm about to be caught with my pants down in here... after I vowed to never let that happen again.

The sound of the doorknob is the same as it was then.

The sound of the front door opening, and being shut.

Except it's your husband this time, instead of my wife... and I'm with you instead of my daughter, in bed.

This is where I change the way it ends. I won't have to *disappear* you, the way I had my wife *disappeared* once she had seen. No, I am the one who will vanish.

No escape but through the window. But first, I have to turn off the light.

This is the darkness that fills the room. The darkness that has left it is me.

The darkness now outside the window.

Watching.

Whispering...

The beginning and end to your dreams.

"Once upon a time..."

Your eyes, now awakened, continue the story.

There was a faithful wife...

You see an empty glass beside you on the nightstand.

Who thought she had a faithful husband...

You see an empty place beside you in bed.

Then, one night...

You see a shape rounding the corner from the hall.

A stranger came along...

You see that the shape is him.

And whispered a fairytale in her ear.

You see him standing in the doorway, peering in.

Later, when her husband entered the room...

The whites of your eyes make him gasp.

She saw him as he really was.

Closing your eyes, you feel a darkness enter the room... for the second time tonight.

This one isn't like the last. You know where this one has come from. You know what its intentions are. You even know its name.

"Henry..." you say. Your agony, voiced. "Where have you been tonight?"

Your eyes stay closed. You listen. Praying...

That his fairytale lies will lull you back to sleep.

Ricardo's Second Coming

There comes a time when a man's gotta stop running. Come out of hiding. Turn back to face the life he left behind.

Four years holed up in this hellhole hick town, and I've been drowning every day without her. Can't believe my coward ass waited this long to come up for air. To finally set out to reclaim what's rightfully mine. The life I should have had with the one I should have been having it with. The one I *will* be having it with before the darkness gives way to dawn.

Or my name ain't Ricardo and she ain't the Magdalena who owns my heart.

—Ricardo, you crazy, man. *Muy loco.* All talking like you gonna go back in time and be with her again. I got news for you, homes. Ain't no time machine been invented yet.

—Don't need no time machine, Marcos. Fuck that. I'm gonna go back to where I came from and find her. That simple. Whatever she may be doing now.

—Man, she probably got a family now. You know she got a man, fine as you say she is. Probably got kids now, too. A lot of things can change in four years.

—Don't matter. Me and her together for life.

—Together? You ain't even seen her since you left that place you grew up in.

—Yeah, but we been together all this time. I know she think about me every day.

—That ain't together, though. I may think about some females I used to be with, but that don't make us together no more.

—It all depends on what you believe. You got to have that belief, see? That faith in what you know in your heart.

—That's that moonshine talking. Either that, or that big ass moon up there. Got you forgetting about your real life. Like Myrna. What you gonna do about her?

—Not *gonna*. Already did.

—Yeah? Let me guess. You finally dumped her?

—You could say that.

—Into a ditch, right? Now where have I heard this one before. Shit kind of twisted. Ain't all that funny.

—Except it ain't no joke this time. You see me laughing?

—I ain't seen you laugh in ages. That don't mean nothing.

—Neither did she. To me. That's what made it easy to do.

—Shit, Ricardo. That's cold. Quit playing, man. Starting to freak me out.

—I ain't playing no more. I'm done playing around in my life.

—Okay, my dude. You officially cut off from the sauce. Time to end this little tailgate and get your ass back home.

—You read my mind. But only if you mean my *real* home. Cuz ain't nothing binding me to this place. Not with Myrna out the picture now. Only one piece of business left before I leave here for good.

—Cut the shit, Ricardo. Seriously. Ricardo?

—Believe what you want. Don't matter to me. What's done is done.

—Tell me you didn't. You ain't really kill her. You ain't really kill her. I mean if she really dead, it was just some kind of accident…

—Won't no accident. I'm through with accidents. *Accident* is what got her ass killed. *Accidentally* gonna have my child. Like she ain't planned the whole thing to keep my ass here forever. I ain't having that. That ain't the life I wanted. That ain't the life I'm supposed to have in this lifetime.

—You officially off the deep end. Face redder than this here Camaro. Probably off those meds and hallucinating some shit up is all I can figure. Till you even got me starting to believe this sick-ass shit you saying. What in the actual fuck?

—I ain't hallucinating. I'm seeing more clearly than ever. And speaking of colors. You the one turning yellow, Marcos.

—Gone and killed her ass after four years. And she pregnant, too? Nuh-uh. Can't be. No way can it be.

—Had to be. Had to be. No choice. She left me no choice.

—Even killed that little fetus up inside her. *Your* fetus, man.

—That's right. That's what it's like when you going off to a new life. No choice but to cut off old ties. Even if it take a real blade like this one to do it.

—Oh, I see. So now you gonna pull a blade on me, bro? Like, really?

—Lighten up, Marcos. It's only life and death. Minus the life part. So mostly just the death. Now relax and let this blade take you home.

Time can't kill the heart, no matter how hard it tries. That's what my mamá used to tell me.

A lot can happen in four years. Old loves can die. New loves can be born. Anything you can imagine. It's all possible if it's the heart.

El corazón. No wonder the word's got that masculine article in front of it. It's the heart of the man that suffers the most. Like mine, ever since my Magdalena left me.

We used to have this chemistry that lit fires in the sky. We used to have these fights that brought the world crashing down. My world crashed down when she ended things. I honestly wanted to take her life then and there. But I knew we'd be together again someday. I knew we'd never stop thinking about each other in the however-long-it-took for us to reunite.

I've seen her face in the faces of the other women since. Like Myrna. She was the closest I could find to Magdalena. Same frame. Similar fire inside. But not the same. I was just pretending they were sisters or something. But they weren't. Not even close. Neither was the love we had. It couldn't hold a candle to the love between Magdalena and me.

We used to have this thing between us, me and her. No words needed. Ever since the first time we ever saw each other from opposite sides of the street. Two wild animals answering each other's mating calls. Our bodies blocking the traffic. Horns trying to honk us out the road, but we didn't give a fuck. We started taking off our clothes right there. Now the horns were honking to cheer us on. Two crazy kids fucking in the middle of the street. Like two street cats. Not a word yet said between us.

Time can't kill memories like those.

Marcos was wrong when he said there ain't no time machine. I've been a time traveler four years. *Cuatro años*, man. Going back in my mind every second. Living in the past and shit. Like some science fiction motherfucker. Living in memories. Traveling back, traveling forward. Hypothetical situations in my mind keeping me from moving forward in

NATHANIEL BLACKHELM

my life. Like, what if she still love me? What if? Till one day, there won't no *what if* no more. I started having faith in my mind. She still love me. She made a mistake. She calling out to me to travel across time and find her. To go back to the way we used to be.

Not that there's any real going back. Not in time. I know this is reality. I ain't living in no delusional world like some schizophrenic motherfucker. I took a sledgehammer to the time machine in my mind and destroyed it. The memories had gotten old and cold, man. They'd started to freeze my brain. I didn't need no frozen brain on account of my already frozen heart. So I decided to set out and make a new life with her. To not just imagine it, but make it real. I decided this is reality, but I can still have her. This is the present, but she can still be mine.

Fuck the time machine. The only machine I need to get where I'm going is this here set of wheels. Marcos won't mind. He won't need it where he going. That motherfucker probably already got his own pair of wings by now. Traveling through the past and present and shit. Seeing things from all directions, wherever he is.

Be with me, *amigo*. You the angel on my shoulder for this crazy ass ride.

Time to crank this motherfucker up and get going.

—That shit was cold, Ricardo. Taking my life like that.

—What I'm supposed to do, man? I needed your wheels.

—How the fuck you gonna kill me over a car?

—This ain't no ordinary car, man. This car got memories behind it and shit. Nostalgic value. You know. All those rides we used to take around town.

—What, and you couldn't have just borrowed it?!

—Nah man, it was more than that. I knew you wouldn't come along for the ride I was on. Not for this one. And I needed a friend by my side.

—I ain't your friend no more, Ricardo.

—Come on now. What you mean you ain't my friend?

—What you think? You done went and took my life. Took Myrna's life, too. Like we never even existed. Tried to act like that baby up inside her never existed either. You wrong, Ricardo. You dead wrong, man.

—Hold up, Marcos. *Cállate* for a second. Can't you see I'm trying to merge onto the highway here? Come on, you assholes! You believe these people? Friday night, and they driving like it's a Sunday afternoon!

—Man, you ain't even trying to listen. Just want to hear what you want to hear. No respect for the wisdom of the dead. I'm out of here, Ricardo. I knew this was a mistake.

—Hold up! Damn man, can't a driver get situated? There. Got my course set for the next two hundred fifty miles. Gonna be a straight shot back to the old *barrio*. Now what was you rattling on about?

—Oh, nothing much. You know. Just how your ass should be ashamed for the three *lives* you took tonight.

—I do what I gotta do. That's what separates you from me.

—No, what separates our asses now is life and death. You alive. I'm dead. Myrna's dead. That seed up inside of her's dead. Can you understand the difference between dead and alive?

—I do. I ain't the one confused. That'd be you, all coming back up in here after you murdered and shit.

—*Verdad.* Thanks for reminding me. I was murdered by my own supposed best friend. And for what? Well, let's see here. First you say you getting rid of old ties. Fine. But then you go and call my name, asking me along for the ride. All contradicting yourself. Yeah, Ricardo. Alright. And you say *I'm* the one that's confused.

—You wanna know the real reason I killed you, Marcos?

—I'm dying to know. Actually, that shit's probably the real reason I'm back here talking with you somehow. Coming back into your head and shit for answers.

—Straight up, man. I'll tell you why. Because I knew you loved Myrna more than I did.

—Huh?

—See, I knew you could take better care of her than me. You get it, Marcos? *Marcos?* You still there, man? Done gone dead silent all the sudden.

—*Ricardo.* What you trying to pull, man? Don't you know I can see through your lies?

—Look inside yourself, homes. Then you'll know who's really lying.

—Don't even try this.

—I ain't trying nothing. Only thing I'm trying is to show you something inside your own heart.

—My heart ain't even beating no more.

—Don't matter. Your heart ain't really in your heart, anyway. Not when it belongs to someone else.

—Yeah? That's good, cuz my real heart got a knife through it.

—See? You laughing again. That's good, homes. That's what I like to hear.

—Pretty sure it beats my screaming.

—You ain't lying! Never would've guessed you had that set of lungs.

—Not my finest moment. Yours either, shanking the shit outta me like that. But in all seriousness… how you knew I loved Myrna?

—Hard to miss. Way you would always ask about her. Make sure I was treating her right. You made me care for her even more than I really did. I owe you for that. So does she.

—Is that why you killed me? Cuz if so, I can see that. It was wrong to feel that way about my friend's girl. I knew it. I knew how wrong it was.

—No it wasn't. It won't wrong. That's just it. Won't nothing in the world wrong about it. And I got news for you, homes. She love you, too. Would ask about your ass the same way.

—But you know I never touched her, right?

—Maybe so. But you should have.

—What you mean? If just thinking about her got my ass stabbed, no telling what you'd've done if we'd...

—That ain't what got y'all killed. It won't a punishment. It was a gift. My parting gift to you both. You two done a lot for me these past couple years. Helped me live day to day. Gave me something to get up for in the morning. I shouldn't have stood between you so long. Should have brought your asses together sooner. Some other way. But there won't no other way to do it. Not for you two. Neither one of you live like that. Neither one of you follow your hearts.

—You trying to say that's what this is all about?

—That's what *life* is all about. And I'm sick of living any other way. Ain't you?

—You forget one thing. I ain't actually *living* no more.

—Man, what you talking about? You alive for the first time in your life. Now go and do what you dead for. Find Myrna and be happy. She your true love. I'll bet she thinking of you right now.

—And how you claim to know something like that?

—Same way I know my Magdalena thinking of me. Same way I know she still back where I'm headed. My heart speaks to me. It tells me what I need to know.

—People change though, Ricardo. What if she don't love you no more?

—My heart tell me she do. She tried to kill it, but it ain't die. That's the heart for you. Even when your loved one done killed it, it stay alive. Even *you* got my back on that.

—I got your back on that, at least. But don't be thinking your ass is forgiven. That shit may never happen. Gonna need some serious time on that.

—And don't forget what else it is you need. *Who* else. Myrna. I want to see your asses together soon.

—You *loco*, homes. The most *loco* motherfucker I ever knew.

—*Verdad.* Must be true. The number of times you've said that over the years. The number of times I've heard that said since the day I was born.

Time is a funny thing. Scientists still don't know shit about it. How to alter it. How to travel through it. Yet what I got me here is a genuine time machine. And all it took was a little bit of faith. All I gotta do is keep my foot on the pedal. Don't let up. See obstacles in my path, don't slow down. Just keep on moving toward what I feel inside. Toward the place that has always stayed inside of me.

The closer I get to the old world, the more the laws of the universe change. The more laws of the road I break, the more I break the laws of time. Breaking the speed limit gets me closer to my past, so I don't just break it, I shatter it. Braking cars delay me to my destination, so I dodge them to either side. Fuck *them* if they get run off the highway. Their fault. Not mine.

This is the world at Mach speed. A blur to either side of me, clarity in front. Like I'm driving toward a crystal dimension. Things look shiny there. Things are standing still. They look like they haven't changed in all these years. The shapes of cities. The hearts of men. All as shiny as the day they were born. Shapes as real as I want them to be. Projections, man. Confessions of my hope. But not delusions. Don't call them that. No need to be labeling my ass as schizophrenic. Already told you, I ain't nothing like that.

Truth is, it's just memories I'm driving through. Road hazards they don't put up no signs for. It ain't their fault. They can't, see, cuz they'd be different for everybody. Everybody's memories are different the closer they get to some place their heart used to live. Or in my case, some place their heart never left. It's just the memories and feelings returning to me is all. The real bad ones, the real strong ones that nearly killed me way back when. It just means I'm going in the right direction, being pulled by the right magnetic source.

Her.

El corazón. Who was I kidding? The word ain't masculine. The heart's an object owned by woman. Being pulled by woman. In my case, by the Magdalena who owns my heart.

For too long, my heart ain't been where my heart is. Not in my body. With her. I will forgive her only if she decides to take me back.

—You swerving too much, Ricardo.

—Been swerving damn near the whole trip. Ain't my fault. You the one should've had the alignment fixed, Marcos.

—It ain't the car, homes. It's the maniac behind the wheel.

—Look man, I ain't the one driving this thing. It's on automatic pilot. See? Look what happens when I take my hands off the wheel.

—I wouldn't be doing that.

—And watch what happens when I take my foot off the pedal. Ain't that something? Car keeps going just as fast.

—Pretty sure that's just the cruise control, *ese*.

—Man, whatever. Ain't you learned a thing or two about miracles where you been?

—Huh. Don't I wish. Ain't nothing where I been but a bunch of confusion and darkness.

—You ain't found Myrna yet?

—Man, I ain't found no one. I ain't talked to no one since the last time I talked to you.

—That's funny. I would've thought you'd be hitting it off with her by now. Not to mention hitting that shit.

—Wish I could say I knew what the fuck I'm doing over there. Ain't no one around. No light, no nothing. So I've just spent the last few hours cursing your name.

—Hey, this ain't about me. About what's been done. It's about what's *to* be done. By you. You gotta stay focused on that.

—Whatever, man. I can't even see in front of me over there.

—Then close your eyes and just start walking.

—You mean like the way you drive? Eyes closed, still pressing the pedal? Some good that'll do.

—No kidding, Marcos. That's the new way you gotta live.

—Sounds inspiring. But maybe you should watch the road.

—Who needs to? I got faith, see? My eyes are shut,

but I know I'll get where I need to be. You need to have more faith, my friend.

—*You* need to open your eyes, Ricardo.

—Why's that? When I can see all things without seeing.

—Then you know you're coming in hot off this exit ramp, right?

—This is it. You feel it? The big return. Like re-entering the Earth's atmosphere from outer space.

—Shit Ricardo, this ain't no space shuttle!

—No? Well, we about to fly regardless…

—You really about to launch us off this bridge?

—Nothing like a dramatic entrance to announce my homecoming.

—Fuck this! I'm out before the splashdown. Already died once today.

Underwater is a fearful place. Time is slowed by the water. Things move in slow motion. Breathing stops. You have to rely on the last breath you took. Whether you knew it would be your last breath or not.

I've lived the last few years underwater. I know how to live without breathing. I know how to handle myself down here in the deep.

The river is an ancient world. Things sink to the bottom and become artifacts. Antiques. But it's too dark to see them. Even with the headlights of the car shining down.

The car will become a relic. I will not. I refuse to be damned to the past.

The water doesn't want me down here anyway. It pulls the car down, but pushes me up.

The passenger window is somehow open for me to escape. That's Marcos, always looking out for my ass. Once

I'm through the window, the water does the rest of the work. Things ain't moving in slow motion anymore. Instead I'm shooting to the top like a bullet. Like time is speeding up to make up for lost time. Time spent underwater. The minute just past. The four years of my life before that.

The universe is finally turning in my favor. Repaying what it owes me by bending its own rules. Reversing gravity. Cushioning its hardest blows. Like the impact of the crash. I should be part of the river right now, sinking down instead of being shot up.

I break the surface and find that I've reached my destination. The distant lights of the *barrio* tell me I've returned.

A breath held four years is finally released.

My life, finally picked up where I left it off.

—Nice driving, Ricardo. You really stuck that water landing, homes.

—Whatever, Marcos. Thanks for staying along for the ride.

—Yeah, my bad. Had a little errand to run while you were taking a dip.

—Yeah? What's that?

—Look Ricardo, she ain't make it here yet.

—Who?

—Who you think, man?

—Myrna?

—Yeah, who else.

—So where is she, then?

—She still dying, man. In that ditch you left her in.

—*What?*

—Yeah, apparently you ain't finish the job.

—It must be a mistake. They fucking with you over

there. She dead. *Muy muerto.* I killed her with my own two hands.

—Well, she ain't here yet.

—Then keep looking.

—Ain't no one to look for. *She ain't here.*

—Then what you doing talking to me? Go and find her the way you found me. You know. In the living world.

—To do what? Watch her die?

—Just be with her, man. Give her comfort. Tell her you gonna be able to take care of her as soon as she give up the fight.

—*You* should be doing this, Ricardo. Not *me.* This shit should be on your pair of shoulders.

—Stop making excuses, Marcos. Don't think. Just go and be the man you always wanted to be, with the woman you always wanted to be with.

—Fine, then. Goddamn you, Ricardo. I'm out.

—Hold up. One quick thing. Was thinking maybe you could tell me where my mamá's buried. I always figured she'd be in the graveyard closest to home. That one over there in the distance.

—How come you never told me what you did to your mamá, Ricardo?

—So, you know?

—You find out a lot of shit here you never knew before.

—Then she buried over there in the graveyard for sure?

—She there, alright.

—Have you seen her where you are?

—I ain't looked for her. Why would I? Your life ain't mine. And besides, I been too busy looking for Myrna. Speaking of, I'd better go to her now.

—You ain't gonna help me find the tombstone?

—You drove most of the way here without looking, didn't you? I'm sure you can find it on your own.

—Yeah, but now I'm on foot in the dead of night.

—Well, maybe you should've thought of that before you went and crashed my ride. Later, Ricardo. Oh yeah. And twenty paces north of the cemetery gazebo is where you'll find your mamá's grave. But I ain't tell you that. Just some voice blowing in the wind.

Dieciseis. Diecisiete.

Where you at, mamá? I know you around here somewhere.

Dieciocho. Diecinueve.

Dark as hell out here. But at least I'm getting dried off.

Veinte. This should be it. Where you at? This one over here, maybe? Nope. What about… oh shit, mamá. There you are. Right under my shoe. My bad. Didn't mean any disrespect.

So this is it. This is *it*? Damn, this the best they could do after I left? Damn shame they couldn't do any better. Damn crying shame I couldn't be here to make sure they did. Cuz you deserve better than this little ass gravestone not even sticking up from the ground.

Lo siento, mamá. I'm sorry they didn't give you a better resting place. Sorry I've never visited you here before. Sorry I never bothered saying 'sorry.'

I took it out on you, didn't I? When Magdalena didn't want the baby. I thought it was because you hadn't raised me right. Because you hadn't given me the tools I needed to make things work with her. I thought whatever she wanted that was missing in me was because of you. Because of something you did or didn't do. Something you maybe could have taught me. Some way you had maybe fucked up my life.

The truth is, she left me because I've always been *loco*. And that ain't on you. I can see that now. You were never the one I should have blamed.

When you used to tell me the story of papá, you told it like you had forgiven him the minute he walked out the door. You always said, *he had to follow his heart*. Never mind that I was just a baby up inside who needed a father. You said he never could have been a good father to me if he'd stayed. His heart would've been all twisted up in the woman he loved more than you. I always saw it as you giving up on him too easily. Plus giving up on the life your baby might have had. But now I see things differently. I've come around to a different way of thinking that's a lot like yours.

Follow your heart, you always said. *Help those around you learn to follow theirs.*

I'm finally doing that now. I hope it's not too late for you to be proud.

That last night here, I was blind. Blind and *loco*. Already *loco* from birth, but even more blind than usual. With rage. The worst possible combination for those around me. For the one person who was trying to talk to me. *You.*

I'm still *loco*, but not blind anymore. If only I hadn't been so blind that last night. I really fucked up, didn't I? Doing this to you. I damned you to a place where you have to be alone. Because you have no true love to reunite with where you are.

Tell me: Who *was* your true love in life? Was it papá, a man who didn't love you back? Or worse yet, was it me? Your own son who scapegoated you, stabbed you, burned our house down and ran away?

I've done some bad things in this life. Unforgivable things. But none as unforgivable as what I did to you.

Lo siento. I'm sorry. I came here to say that from the

heart.

But that's not the only reason.

I came here to ask for your blessing. Because soon me and Magdalena will be together again. I'm going to marry her this time. I'm going to do it right. I want you to be there with me in spirit. This time, you really will be a grandmother. I will not let her terminate another child.

Hasta luego. And keep an eye out for someone named Marcos. He'll be bringing in a woman named Myrna soon. They're good people, and maybe they can help ease some of your loneliness.

I'm off to do the same for myself.

—Marcos. You there, man? I'm walking out the graveyard and could use your eyes if you're around. Marcos?

—Marcos ain't here right now.

—Who is this?

—Listen carefully. You don't recognize my voice?

—Myrna? Is that you?

—Yeah, Ricardo. It's me. Your beloved Myrna. The one you left in a ditch to die.

—So he made it to you, then. Marcos. He's with you now.

—Yeah, he made it. He was there for me. Unlike you. You were never really there for me, were you? You were just playing the whole time. Pretending you cared for me. Then when you done with that little game, you up and strangle me like I never meant nothing to you.

—It ain't that you meant nothing to me. It's that someone else meant more. You had the same thing going on with Marcos.

—But that ain't the way to do things, Ricardo. That shit is wrong! You playing like you God, taking people's lives whenever you want. Taking they lives for them to be together. Taking they lives when you ready to be apart.

—So Marcos explained it to you? How I killed the two of you to bring your asses together?

—He did, but I ain't buying it entirely. Cuz you forgetting one thing. The life in me you up and destroyed.

—I thought they'd have a way to fix that there.

—Yeah, well you always was relying on other people to clean up your messes. There ain't no way to fix it, Ricardo. Some things just can't be fixed.

—Then I'm sorry. I'll admit it won't a perfect plan.

—No, Ricardo, it *was* perfect. For *you*. Leaving nothing at all between us so you could go off and have the life you really want.

—It ain't like that.

—Yeah? Then how is it?

—Marcos gonna... hold up. Let me cross this street. Too many damn cars out here tonight. But yeah, like I was saying. Marcos gonna look after you.

—Yeah. *Marcos.* Marcos gonna clean up your mess. You lucky he a better man than you could ever pray to be.

—That's why you two meant to be together. Cuz you a better woman than I was ever supposed to be with.

—Don't be playing those head games with me.

—Like I told Marcos, I'm done playing games in my life. I'm here to find the woman I'm supposed to be with.

—What was *I*, then? A distraction? A way to pass the time?

—No. More like a casualty of the way I used to live.

—How many more casualties, Ricardo? That's the question on everybody's lips where I'm at.

—Tell them: as many as it takes to get it right.

—You tell them yourself. Why don't you be man enough to take your own life? Instead of tearing everyone else's apart. All you gotta do is step out in front of one of those cars passing by. Just think of how many lives you'd save.

—Can't do that. Got too much living to do. Besides, I know I wouldn't end up where you are.

—It ain't too late to redeem yourself. To start over. Start anew.

—You're right. And that's what I'm back here to do. Start over. Starting from the place I was born. My old house. I want to see what became of it after I left.

—You mean after you burned it down with your mother inside? Funny how you think you know someone, but you don't. Not really, anyway. Turns out I never really did know you, Ricardo. I mean, not about your mother or this... Magdalena. You was always just hiding your past from me.

—It won't just you. I was hiding it even from myself sometimes. But it's too late to change any of that. Whole reason I'm here is to move forward, not back. So if you'll excuse me, I have a new beginning or two left to make before the end of the night.

The old *barrio* is a living snapshot. Same ruin. Same decay. Same old fiends out past the deadliest hours of night. These were the hours I used to see my Magdalena—the hours we used to feel the most alive. I imagine she never left. Not without a life-or-death reason to. Murder was mine. Two of them, actually. The fetus she killed when she had the abortion. My own mother I killed in my rage. It all sounds so disconnected now. So illogical. Time will do that to old ways of thinking.

Maybe I'm not as *loco* as before.

Maybe the *barrio* isn't either. I'm not hearing any

animal cries to answer to. Figures pass, but looking downward. Not looking in my eyes. They must know a predator when they see one. The cars are afraid to honk, even though I'm walking in the middle of the street. The same street where me and her first met. You'd think they'd have a shrine here or something. They do that sort of thing for big events in some places. But not here. Not in a place like this.

The few blocks between the street we originally met on and the street I grew up on pass so quickly, they may as well not even exist.

This should be the place. An empty lot where mamá's ashes are preserved. Where no one would dare build in all these years since the fire. Because it's sacred ground to the one who burned it down. Me.

My eyes can't believe the desecration. The newly built house on the lot where mamá's used to be. How dare they betray me. My eyes. Whoever did this. How dare they betray me like this.

A light comes on in the window of the house. There is a figure standing there. Unreal.

Dawn is near. So is the end of my journey.

For she is in there.

Through the window.

Magdalena.

Somehow.

—Ricardo. My son. It has been a long time.

—Mamá?

—*Sí, mijo.* It is me.

—What are you doing here?

—You are standing in front of the place I never left.

—But I thought you were in…

—No, *mijo.* I have been *here* all along. Waiting

patiently for you to return.

—But why, mamá? Why would you wait for me?

—It's like I always told you: time can't kill the heart, no matter how hard it tries. I've been watching this place for you all this time. Because I knew you'd want to know what went on here. And also…

—Also what?

—Also because we can't be together after this. When all is said and done. Because of certain things you've done. A certain way you've lived.

—I ain't done yet. Living. In fact, I ain't even started. It starts with her. That's why I came back. Without even knowing where to start looking. But something told me to start right here.

—Pretty funny, eh? That she would choose this place to build her new life. Especially when no one else would. They all knew what had happened here. A mother murdered by her son. Who would want her ashes—*my* ashes—haunting the space beneath their feet? But she had always wanted a home. A baby, too. Just not by you, it seems. Remember that fateful night? I'll never forget how devastated you were. *Mamá, I found out she was pregnant but she ain't keep it. Said she can't be having no loco child.* She has tried her best to ignore the history here. The part she played in it. But in her own way, she still thinks of you all the time.

—Is she alone?

—You'll have to find that out for yourself. Keep looking through the window. *There.* Did you see him?

—I saw him. *Sí.* I just saw him pass by.

—They are married, *mijo.* They have their own life. Their own child. See the light there at the end of the house? That's their baby's room. Their infant son. He has just woken up and they are tending to him. Only, they are foolish to leave their curtains open. It's as if they have nothing to hide.

—She is as beautiful as she ever was. Even more.

—Catch your breath. You're hyperventilating.

—I can't. Can't breathe…

—Look away from the window. Don't take it too hard.

—No. No way to stop looking. Too glorious in the light. Naked. Just for me.

—No, *mijo*. Just foolish. Foolish to linger like that wearing nothing. Look away, before you go crazy. Run away, before she sees you here.

—No. Too late. She knows I am here. She wants me here. I can feel her inviting me in.

—*Mijo*, what are you doing?

—Exactly what she wants me to.

—But your clothes! Where are you going like that?

—Back into the house that is rightfully mine. Back into the place I was born.

—*Mijo*, no! You mustn't do this! *Mijo*!!

The door is wood. I'm hard as metal. Nothing can stop me from breaking in.

My house. Not his. *He* is the burglar. The stranger who stole my rightful life.

I break down the door with all my might.

On their TV, two animals charge each other in the wild. In their living room, the same, him and me.

Naked. Primal. Both fighting over the same female mate.

Roaring. Clashing. Recoiling. Charging again.

He knows what I am here to do. She is mine.

His eyes refute it. *Mine*, they say. But he knows. He knows in his heart my love is stronger than his, just as his neck knows my grip is stronger than his breath.

She is mine, and she will always be mine.

His eyes no longer refute it. They go blind. As blind as they were to have never seen me coming. To have never known I never even left.

This is *my* house. She. *She* is my house. Inside of her is the place I was born.

The place I will be resurrected.

Before dawn's first light.

—Well, well, well. You proud of yourself… Ricardo? That's your name, isn't it?

—Who the fuck is this?

—Someone you never took the courtesy to formally meet.

—Sorry. Voice not ringing any bells.

—The man you just killed, you son of a bitch.

—That was fast.

—Well, it only takes a second to die. To destroy a life. Whereas to build one up takes a lifetime. Congratulations, motherfucker. You just stole everything I ever had.

—Wrong. You never had it. You never had *her*. She is and always will be mine.

—I saw your eyes saying that. But I saw no love in them. Just insanity. There's a difference, you know.

—Think so?

—I know so.

—You think you know something, huh?

—I know more than you will ever know.

—Yeah? Like what?

—Like how it feels like to have a life with her. To have a baby by her.

—Why you mother-… if you weren't already dead, I

would…

—That's all you know how to do, isn't it? Destroy what other people have built.

—You don't know me.

—I learned everything there was to know about you in the minute you destroyed *me*.

—You don't know about me and Magdalena.

—That's where you're wrong. She told me about you. She and I didn't have any secrets.

—Then you should have known I was coming all along.

—I prefer not to live my life in fear.

—Well, look at where that way of living got you.

—Like yours has gotten you somewhere better. Are you proud?

—This is exactly where I want to be.

—So be it, then. Do what you will. My eyes will be closed. So long as you send her up to me, I don't care. So long as you send our baby, too.

—You'll be closing your eyes a long time before that happens.

—She will never give in to you.

—Keep your eyes open, because we'll see about that.

We used to have this thing between us, Magalena and me. No words needed.

It happens again as we see each other across the wreckage of the room. The wreckage of an age spent apart. No words. No explanations. We move toward each other across the fabric of time. Past. Present. Future. All colliding. Exploding. Becoming one.

Impossible. Impassable: the distance between us. So much so that only a bullet could traverse it. A bullet fired from the gun I hadn't expected to be in her hands.

We never make it back into each other's arms.

A baby is crying. A now fatherless baby. Only now can I see what I have done.

She has shot me through the heart. For real this time. I should have killed her the first time around. But I couldn't. She's the only one I could never hurt. The only life in this world I could never take.

I've taken everything from her life now.

I'm sorry. Magdalena. I'm sorry for what I've done.

I know I'm going to hell for all of this.

Sex Crime Symphony

In memory of Angella Wilz (1979 – 1994)

Shathunk, goes the rope as it catches.

Kersnap, goes her neck.

Swashtakoom! comes the lightning from the sky.

These are the sounds the ape-like creatures hear in the moment they are born. The moment the lightning animates them from the dirt of the forest floor.

In that first moment, they are blind. Then their eyes open to a darkened forest. A blinding light flashes above. *Swashtakoom!* They recognize the sound from the moment of their birth. From the energy burst that imbued them with life seconds earlier.

The blinding light illuminates the figure hovering above them. She is wearing the color of the lightning. Blinding white.

She is flying. Floating. Or rather, swinging back and forth. Her body dangling by the rope around her neck.

So this is the world into which they've been born.

Their consciousness pedals them backwards to the tragedy's start.

Thump a thump a thump a.

This is what the rapist hears.

Thump a thump a thump a.

The sound in his head when he rapes.

And he hears it the first moment he lays eyes on Angie Wilkes. And he knows she will become his next prey.

She knocks at the door as he is crossing through his brother's living room.

Thump a thump a thump thump thump.

Double take. A white flash had caught his eye. He stops and turns toward the girl in the white t-shirt standing behind the screen door. He keeps his eyes on the white t-shirt and the youthful face above it as he approaches the door to let her in.

"Can you get that, Alex?" calls a male voice from down the hall.

"Already there." He presses the handle open. "So you're the babysitter, eh? Name's Alex. Charlie's brother. The one who's taking him out tonight." He forms the words with his mouth and hopes the sounds are coming out clearly. But he can no longer hear himself talk. He can't hear anything over the *thump a thump a thump a* beating inside his head.

"Nice to meet you. I'm Angie," her young lips say.

She extends her hand and he accepts it, shaking it, keeping it in his until she pulls it away and steps into the house. His two young nephews come ambling into the room, followed by his brother Charlie.

"Hi Angie," Alex sees Charlie's mouth say. "Thanks for watching these guys tonight. We shouldn't be out past midnight." Then he feels Charlie's hand on his shoulder, leading him out of the house, down the porch steps, out to the truck. Alex gets into the driver's seat and looks back through the rear windshield, but doesn't see the girl anymore. The *thump a thump a thump a* beats softer in his head as the house recedes from view in the rearview mirror. He finds he can hear his own voice again as they turn onto the road leading into town.

"How old is she, Charlie?" Alex asks his brother.

"Fifteen, I think. Why?"

"Just asking. Man, I've got a splitting headache."

"You're in trouble, then. We're not even at the bar yet."

Thump a thump a. Thump a thump a.

The rhythm in Alex's head doesn't stop at the bar. It throbs steadily over Charlie's lamentations about the divorce settlement and his every-other-weekend visiting privileges with the two boys. It throbs steadily down into Alex's other head as he thinks of the Angie girl babysitting his nephews right now in the house where he is staying as a weekend guest.

"Have another," he keeps telling Charlie. "Have another."

Several hours later, he slips in the question. "Does the babysitter live far from you?" Charlie doesn't ask him why he asks about the babysitter this time. The alcohol in him just answers:

"No. Only a few blocks away."

"What street?" Alex asks the alcohol in his brother.

"Edgar Lane," the alcohol slurs.

Alex keeps one hand on his glass and the other hand rubbing against one or the other of his two throbbing heads as Charlie slowly drinks himself unconscious. Then it is time for Alex to drive them home. The throbbing gets louder and louder in his heads the closer they get to the house.

Thump a thump a thump thump thump.

The sound startles Angie awake with a gasp. She vaults herself up from the couch in Charlie's living room she hadn't given herself permission to fall asleep on earlier. The clock says 2:02 a.m.

Thump a thump a thump thump thump. She hurries across the living room to answer the knock at the door. Alex barges past her carrying Charlie and dumps him onto the couch still warm from her sleep.

"Old Charlie had one too many tonight," Alex says. "But don't worry, he told me to take you home."

"I should probably call my mom first," she says, still orienting herself to the scene.

"But isn't she already asleep? I mean, don't you think it's too late to call her?"

She thinks about her mom having to get up for work in the morning. About how her mom might get mad at Charlie (her mom's former coworker at the mill) for making her get out of bed and drive over this late at night. What if her mom wouldn't let her babysit for Charlie anymore? That'd be one less way to save up for a car by the time she got her license. *Charlie. Why did you do this to me, Charlie?* she thinks as she glares at his sleeping face on the couch.

"Come on," urges Alex from the doorway. "Let's get going." He steps out the door before she can respond. As she emerges onto the porch, she sees him crossing the short distance to the end of the road, where a guardrail stands in front of the woods.

"Where are you going?"

"Shhhhhh," he hisses, putting his finger to his lips. "Remember, the boys are sleeping."

"Aren't we driving?"

"Better not, in my condition. Besides, I know an even faster way."

"But do you know where I live? I'm all the way over on Edgar Lane."

"I know. Charlie told me. I used to live around here. Everywhere connects." He continues past the guardrail into the woods and starts to vanish.

"Wait. Where are you going?" She runs out past the guardrail and stops in front of the trees. His figure emerges from the vanishing point with his hand outstretched.

"Come on," he says. "Take my hand and follow me." He takes her hand *for* her and pulls her into the darkness of the woods.

"Wait," she says, her hand being pulled by his. Her feet, not knowing whether to pedal forward or back. "I can't see."

"Don't worry," he says, tugging her along through the trees. "I *can*."

"Wait," she says, her feet pedaling wildly. "Please wait."

"I've waited long enough." He pulls her hard and lifts her pedaling feet off the ground. His hand covers her mouth. His other hand reaches under her skirt and tears at the thin fabric that covers her other mouth. He lifts her entire body up and runs with it while her muffled scream sounds deeper and deeper into the woods.

And his head goes *thump a thump a thump a* as he runs.

And his other head goes *thump a thump a thump a*, making it hard for him to run.

And as he nearly trips over the ladder to a deer stand, he decides: *This place will do just fine.*

He slams her down hard onto the dirt. Slams himself down hard upon her, his hand still covering her mouth.

And the instrument sounds deep into the forest. *Hmmmm. Hummmmoana. Hmmmmm.*

And the instrument sounds deep into her head. *Hmmmm. Hummmmoana. Hmmmmm.*

The instrument of her muffled screams.

In his own head, percussion hammers over it.

Thump a thump a thump a. Thump a thump a thump a.

The symphony ends.

She looks up to see his shape towering over her. Even higher, a shape towers over *him*. The outline of a platform extending from a tree. A deer stand.

A figure hangs by a rope from the deer stand.

Blinding white.

His hand pulls her up from the dirt of the forest floor.

The whiteness of her t-shirt ruined.

The blinding white figure above them not really there. Just somewhere in the back of her mind.

The man who just violated her. Really there.

His hand really leading her back through the woods.

His truck really driving her home.

Home.

The shower lever turns. The doorknob to her room turns.

She makes sure not to wake her mother up on her way in.

Crank. Buzz. Whir. Clunk.

The workings of the human justice machine.

Crank. Buzz. Whir. Clunk.

Malfunctional when it comes to punishing rape.

The system works (doesn't work) like this.

A rape gets put into the machine. A rape sentence gets spit out.

Kerplunk.

Two years. Maybe four. A maximum of ten.

And yet.

A rape gets put into a girl. A death sentence gets spit out.

Kersnap.

There goes the victim's will to live.

Angie Wilkes knows this truth all too well. She is no longer living, inside.

She showers and changes clothes three or four times a day. Sleeps way more than she used to. No longer cares about getting her license. No longer makes good grades in school.

Crank. Buzz. Whir. Clunk.

A machine that no longer functions. Because of rape.

A bottle of pills gets put into the machine. A bottle of pills gets spit out. Pumped out of her stomach by the emergency crew at the hospital. When she awakens, she says she did it so she wouldn't have to testify. She is terrified of facing her attacker in court. The District Attorney stops pushing so hard for a trial. He hates to compromise, but what can he do.

Alex Goodman pleads no contest to second degree sexual assault. At the hearing, his brother Charlie speaks in his favor. He says with a straight face that Alex Goodman is a *good man.* That to his knowledge, he has never committed such a crime before (no *reported* incidents, anyway, Charlie's conscience reminds him), and never would again.

Alex Goodman is sentenced to two years in prison.

Crank. Buzz. Whir. Clunk.

A year passes.

A request for parole is put into the machine. A granting of parole is spit out.

Human justice spits Alex Goodman back out into the civilized world.

Kerplunk.

His brother is there to catch him. To take him into his home. Only a few blocks away from Angie Wilkes'.

Home.

The shower lever turns. The doorknob to her room turns.

The figure in the shower lets the water beat over her. The figure in her room reaches under the bed for the rope.

The first figure prays for a peaceful end. The second figure prays for the strength to bring it about.

The two figures converge in the hall.

They are one and the same.

Angie Wilkes. And the figure in blinding white.

It is a year and a half after the crime. A year after the sentencing.

The deer stand awaits. Her testimony is long in the making.

She is finally ready to take the stand.

Her mother is asleep. She makes sure not to wake her up on her way out.

Wheeeeeee. A gust of air blows through the trees, rustling her white nightgown as her body sways from the deer stand. *Wheeeeeee*, the wind whistles.

Wheeeeeee, the ape-like creatures hear her voice whistle as a little girl. She is a child swinging on the tree swing behind her house. *Wheeeeeee! Mommy, push me higher!* she cries.

And they understand why she chose to hang herself in white. They were born from that sanctity that was stolen from her.

Their consciousness pedals them forward and back.

Krakow! A gunshot startles the ape-like creatures into a daylight scene. They see the image of a hunter perched atop the platform of a deer stand. He has fired once at a grazing fawn below. The fawn slumps down, its face dropping into the dirt.

Bullseye! The hunter climbs down to bag his prey.

The image changes, the scene repeats.

Bullseye! They see the rapist climb down to bang his prey.

And his head goes *thump a thump a thump a.*

And his other head goes *thump a thump a thump a.*

And her muffled scream goes *hmmm hummoana hmmmm.*

And he thinks she's saying *hmmmm ohhh baby yeah.*

This is his dream. The one he's having right now on his brother Charlie's living room couch. The one their consciousness has found a way inside of. The ape-like creatures are inside Alex's dream the same way he has been inside the women he has violated. And he doesn't like the feeling of someone being inside him. But there is nothing he can do to push them away.

Bwa ha ho ha, they laugh. Such a feeble rapist mind they have landed inside of. To put it in his terms: like a pussy not worth the fuck.

Fuck a hump a fuck a hump a fuck a hump a. What crazy rhythms. To think, that's all there is in his head!

The rapist hears laughter in his dream. His own, directed against him. "The fuck are you laughing at?" he calls out from his sleep. Charlie stops to look at him as he walks by the living room couch. Glares at his sleeping face. Regrets having advocated for him. Regrets letting him stay here now. Chuckles in disgust at his freeloading rapist brother.

"My own stupidity," Charlie replies to the sleep-talked question.

The rapist doesn't wake up. He falls into an even deeper sleep. Pulse slowing down. Head slowing down even slower than it already is. And his rhythm goes: *Thump. Thump. Thuuuuump.*

A final heartbeat. Sneak preview. Then the ape-like creatures disconnect and leave his dream.

A blinding white light resets his sleep: the flash of lightning outside the window. The same blinding white light that reorients the ape-like creatures to the forest, that reorients them to her figure hanging above.

Their consciousness has pedaled them back to her. She's been hanging up there far too long.

Bring her down for the mourning! the ape-like creatures collectively pronounce.

Down she is lowered. A blinding white bolt of lightning being lowered in slow motion from the sky. Suspended before it reaches the ground. Halted and harnessed in gentle hands.

They do not let her body touch the dirt. They make sure to keep her death garment unsoiled. They hold her in their collective arms and cradle her. They rock her gently to and fro and sing her a mournful song that lasts all night.

And it goes, *Hummm hummoana hummm. Hummoana hummm hummm hummm.*

Their ceremony is interrupted by the sound of the approaching world.

Hum uh nuh fuck uh nuh hum uh nuh fuck uh nuh

Intruders. The night has already come and gone.

Raise her up for the morning! the ape-like creatures collectively pronounce.

Up she is raised. All the way back up into the trees.

This is how they had found her, hanging from the deer stand. This is how they leave her for the approaching world to find. (No one can know they found her first. No one can know of their existence.)

This is how the hunters find her at daybreak.

This is how the authorities find her in the morning sun.

This is the sound they make as they approach: *Crank. Buzz. Whir. Clunk. Clunk.*

This is the sound of the civilized world's pronouncement concerning her death: *Crank. Buzz. Whir. "Suicide."*

And yet it was murder. Murder to all who fathom the crime. Murder like any rape.

"She was murdered the night it happened," her mother tells the off-screen reporter. "It just took her this long to die." ("*That was what her daughter had meant to say with her final act*," the reporter narrates in voice-over.)

Bwah ha ho, ha.

The rapist cackles in disbelief at the clip on the local news.

"Well, fuck *me*," he says to no one. There is no one there to say it to. His brother has left the house to drink away his heavy conscience. Leaving *him* to converse with the living room couch. "I mean shit, she didn't have to take it so hard. So *hard*. Get it?"

"Get fucked," replies the living room couch.

Humm hummoana hummmm.

The mother turns on the vacuum a few blocks over.

Humm hummoana hummmm.

It begins to pick up the broken pieces.

Hummmmmmmmmmmmmmmmmmmmmmmmmmmmm

Click.

The vacuum is shut off.

The TVs are shut off.

It is time for the sleepy town to sleep.

Even rapists need sleep. They are only animals, after all. Their eyelids grow heavy, even if their consciences do not. Even if their hearts do not. Even if they have no hearts.

Terrapa! That is what it would sound like if a rapist's chest were being torn open. *Terrapa!* But no *thump a thump a thump*.

And yet the rapist hears a *terrapa!*, and a *thump a thump a thump*, and in that moment, is awakened from his sleep. He gasps and looks down at his chest. No damage. Exhales relief and looks down at his erection, thinking some damage needs to be done. For in his head he hears the familiar *thump a thump a thump a* that tells him new prey is somewhere near.

The animal drum is both outside and inside of him. He follows the rhythm inside, out. Running blindly out of the house, past the guardrail at the end of the street, into the woods.

Instinct takes over. A new kind of instinct. Blind. One that tells him what's near without seeing. One that can lead him by rhythm to exactly what he wants.

A receptacle as young and sweet and new as hers was under the deer stand that night.

Deep into the trees the rhythm runs him. Deeper and deeper, till he can no longer see anything at all. Till he can finally only hear—

Thump thump. Thump thump. Thump thump.

The beating of a heart. Not his. Less primal.

Thump thump. Thump thump. Thump thump.

He can no longer hear the rhythm in his head. The rhythm has become the beating heart.

And it goes, *Thump thump. Thump thump. Thump thump.*

The heartbeat multiplies and becomes a chorus. He recognizes the sound as the one that drew him in. The one he fears has led him asunder. For there is no prey to be found unless it's—

Thuuuuump. Something drops inside him. Shapes move in the dark around him. He can sense them closing in on him. *He* is the prey.

The chorus of heartbeats crescendos. *Thump thump! Thump thump!*

Swashtakoom!

He sees them in the flash of light. Massive. Ape-like. Their powerful hands prying open their own chests. The monstrous hearts within their *terrapa*'d rib cages fully exposed to the elements and beating the most violent of blinding whites.

Beating, *thump a thump a thump a thump a thump a thump a—*

Swashtakoom!

A bolt of lightning strikes the deer stand above him, setting it aflame.

The fire lights the silhouette of a hanging figure. The astral scar of the girl who had hanged herself there. The girl who would never lead a full life because of him. Angie Wilkes.

The creatures raise their arms in supplication.

Swashtakoom!

A bolt of lightning strikes one of his two heads. The lower one. Incinerating the fabric and flesh between his legs and crumpling him to his knees.

A deafening scream pierces the woods. Pain and lament, made sound. It is the shrieking wail of a man who can no longer rape.

The creatures raise their arms in supplication.

Swashtakoom!

A bolt of lightning strikes the other of his two heads. The one atop his neck. It deep-fries his cranium and collapses him into a lifeless heap.

Silence envelops the forest in the wake of his demise.

A soft, soundless snow begins to fall. Flake by fluttering flake. It outlines the shape of a girl whose figure is no longer hanging. She materializes, as if from the ether, walking forward through the trees. As she approaches, the ape-like creatures bow before her in a gesture of reverence. They honor the fearless journey she took towards a death imbued with meaning. They celebrate her as a fellow legend whose tragedy has now been avenged.

Her resplendent, snow-dusted form departs as quickly as it had arrived. As quickly and resplendently as a bolt of lightning.

The snow continues to fall. By morning, it will have covered the forest in a sheen of blinding white. And the ape-like creatures will have long since returned to the dirt of the forest floor.

A King Among Beggars

Pimpin' wasn't easy. I didn't have the heart for it. All the bitch-slappin' started to get to me after a while. Started to taint my soul. Not to mention my relationship with the Man Upstairs, who nearly bitch-smote my ass for all the brutality. I could feel His wrath churning, His back turning on me more every day: the hardcore pimpin' life wasn't to His liking. Moreover, I knew it wasn't my true destiny. I had to get right with my Lord and Savior, not to mention my own damn self, so I went into a new line of work. Helping the needy. The beggar folk of my very own community. And I'm the best at what I do, you'd best believe.

See, I'm an entrepreneur at heart. Out here on these streets, you gotta have the heart of an entrepreneur to survive. To figure out a way to eat without getting eaten. How else you think beggar folk get to begging, or someone like me get to becoming a pimp in his past life? Streets force you to compromise and cash in on whatever it is you can. Fuck dignity. Fuck pride. Pretty soon you either pimp-slappin' some hoes into giving better head or you holding a beggar's cup in your hand. I ain't afraid to say I've done both, and didn't like neither one. But I needed both experiences to do what I do now. Funny how things work out.

True destiny is a matter of personal evolution. My own true destiny is with the begging kind. Beggars. Bums. Hobos. Tramps. I rep them, see. Kind of like a Hollywood agent reps big stars. And you gotta admit, they are kind of like stars. The eccentric behavior. The instant recognizability. They're like the icons of your everyday life. You see them out on the street corner, some of them for years. Those are the legends. Others aren't so lucky and fade from sight and memory. Lose their shine. Fall on hard times and disappear from the limelight. Same way I had, just after quitting the pimpin' game.

Back when I quit pimpin', I didn't know what I was gonna do. My leap of faith had led me straight off a cliff. That first night away from the game, I was already down to my last dollar. I bought a soda with it, not a drink—one of the vices of my former pimpin' life—guzzled it down, and found myself with an empty cup in my hand and nowhere to sleep, since I had renounced my former pimpin' quarters (along with the stable of hoes housed therein). I awoke the next morning on a bench in the middle of the city with the cup in my hand no longer empty. It was jingling now, full of change. I swear that must have been the Hand of God that dropped that change in, because it changed the course of my life from that point on.

I started begging to get by, but my heart wasn't really in it. I couldn't stay interested or something. Kept wanting to come up with new sales pitches, different variations on the same old routine. Ways to shake things up and keep myself and the passerby intrigued and entertained. Wanted to try on different personas, play different parts, parts other than the "Former Pimp in Search of Salvation" role I felt I was running into the ground. But the public liked consistency, I found. Didn't necessarily want fixed what wasn't broken, so long as you had a good enough concept and presentation.

I could have kept on panhandling and made out okay. But I looked around and saw my brothers and sisters in the spare change game struggling. So many just never had their acts together from the start. Like this one dude I met early on, went by the name of Breech. Told me he was pulling in less than a dollar a day and couldn't figure out why. I thought something had caught my eye earlier in our conversation and asked him to turn around. That's when I noticed dude had his ass hanging out of a hole in the back of his pants. I mean, something as simple as that had been holding him back all this time. Keeping him from his earning potential. That one gaping hole (or maybe two) reminded me of another: the hole in the market I could potentially fill.

And *bam*, like that, a new business model was born. It occurred to me that I could offer my management services to struggling beggar folk for a portion of their daily earnings. Breech paved the way, and under the guidance of yours truly, started pulling in ten times more than he ever had before. And that was even on the several days I caught him with his ass hanging back out of his pants.

Word spread fast, and so did my reputation for greatness. Ten clients became twenty. Became forty. And the roster just kept on growing. Wasn't long before I assumed my throne as the undisputed king of all who panhandle on these mean and meaningful streets.

My clients are like jesters. They entertain me and speak the truth with their folly. The truth about struggle and profit. Life.

So you think you know something about the world of beggary? Mistah P'll prove you wrong on that. One of them pro bono things I do on occasion. Take sheltered people like yourselves along on my daily rounds in the hours before the shelter line forms. The hours when there are profits to be made and triumphs of the spirit to be witnessed in all their glory. Little enlightenment. Little entertainment. Couple laughs, maybe. Lucky you.

First stop on today's itinerary is Mickey D's. Heroin Man's territory. A somewhat risky placement, McDonald's being a family establishment and Heroin Man being your average neighborhood junkie. Friendly Neighborhood Junkie, I might add, in case that distinction means anything to you superhero fans out there.

Everyone needs a gimmick, see.

Heroin Man's is that he wears a cape and has superpowers. The cape part is easy—just a blanket tied around his neck, same American flag blanket he sleeps under every night. But the superpowers part is a little harder when you don't have the budget for special effects.

Enter target audience: the little tykes who come with the special effects already built up into they precious little heads.

You gotta love tykes, man. Future of society and all, yeah, but besides that, them little midgets got a hell of a lot of faith in the wonders of this world. Don't need no outward show of superpowers to believe they right there up your sleeve. Long as you got the cape on, they on board for the ride. It ain't like you lying. Lying's when you mislead and deceive. Telling them dude's got superpowers ain't a lie because their little minds have already beat you to that assumption once they saw the cape. They already 90% there before you even opened your mouth to give the pitch. They *want* dude to have superpowers. They *need* dude to have superpowers. But when they find out dude done *lost* his superpowers—that's the pitch we use for Heroin Man, see— they gonna do anything their little hearts can to convince they mama to make a donation to the *Get-Mr.-Superhero's-Powers-Back Fund.* When mama roll her eyes and try to hurry them past, they gonna start throwing a fit. May even take what little change they have in their own pockets and run back across the parking lot to throw it into the cup. Mama may know this dude's a junkie without hope, with a blanket tied around his neck, for God's sake, but to them little tykes, he's a superhero under an evil spell that only they can help break in order to save the day.

That's tykes for you, man. Gotta love 'em. Especially when they hand over the silver and green.

NATHANIEL BLACKHELM

Old folks, though? Slightly different demographic. Now I respect my elders and all, knowing I'm gonna become one in a little over a minute, but them geriatrics is a little more selective when it comes to their charitable spendings. One thing's for certain: when it comes to Heroin Man, they definitely ain't buying the superhero bit. With them, you gotta change your strategy and cater to *their* idea of what a true superhero is: someone who's fought for their country. A living embodiment of the time-honored values of honor and sacrifice. Quite simply, they want to see the vet with the missing limb. Which is why I've changed up my strategy with Heroin Man today.

As it turns out, there's a commemorative event over at the War Museum, which usually brings out the old-timers in droves. They're early risers, so they should be filing in for they Egg McMuffins by now. Wonder how H-Man's holding up. Only thing that worries me is we didn't spend enough time prepping for his new role as a vet. Guy's brain is fried, so he's got very little short-term memory to work with. Took me damn near a month to drill the superhero bit into his skull, but on this one, I've had to move a lot faster. Short notice on the special event thing, you feel me?

From the looks of it, I may have rushed things a bit. See for yourself. Dude's sitting over there on the bench, flag (or rather, flag-patterned blanket) all up under his ass, same number of limbs as the plastic Ronald McDonald he's sitting beside: four, when he's supposed to have only three. No good. Shit kind of embarrassing. Will you excuse me for a minute? Gonna need to handle this. Your tour guide'll be right back.

"H-Man. What the fuck is you doin'?"

"Muh-Muh-Mistah P. What you doin' here?"

"What you think, fool? I'm checkin' up on your sorry ass. See you already done fucked up the routine. Got your arm all up out your sleeve and shit. You supposed to be an amputee, fool. How the *'Amputee'* sign gonna work if your arm all up out your sleeve?"

"Buh-buh-but it itches, Muh-Mistah P. I needs to get me some sh-sh-shit soon."

"Fool, what? That ain't my muhfuckin' problem. How much paper you earn so far?"

"Juh-juh-just a duh-duh-duh-duh…"

"A dollar? Fool, you earn a dollar and have the nerve to…"

"… duh-duh-duh-dime! Just a duh-duh-duh-dime!"

"A *dime*? Fool, you earn a dime this whole morning? The fuck you been doin'?! The fuck went wrong?! Was you tellin' 'em the story or not?"

"Yuh-yuh-yessir… buh-buh-been tellin' 'em I'm a vuh-vuh-vet, just like you said!"

"A vet what, fool?"

"A vuh-vuh-veterin… a vuh-vuh-veterin… ah… ah…"

"And what, no one stopped to give you change?"

"… ah … ah … *aria*n! A veterin*arian*!!"

"A veterah-… fool, you's about the stupidest mofo I ever known! It's *veteran*! *Veteran*, fool! Now say it back to me. *Ve-ter-an*."

"Vuh-vuh-veteran. *Veteran*."

"Good. Now put that arm back up in your sleeve and don't be pullin' that shit out again. You'd better start making some Ronald McDonald Telethon type of progress out here or else I'mma make you a real life amputee. Is that clear? Now get the fuck back out to your spot before I turn your dumb ass inside out."

"Yuh-yuh-yessir."

There. Back now. Sorry about that. I swear, the shit I gotta put up with sometimes.

Check it. A message for all the young tykes out there. This is your brain. That was your brain on drugs. Any questions?

Figured some of y'all might have a few after witnessing that little exchange.

Like why Mistah P gotta be so damn hard on his people? Some of y'all ain't used to seeing folks get they asses handed to them like that. Well, let me tell you something—and remind myself, too. Can't be having no sidewalk version of the streets. Don't be thinking that just because I manage beggars, I can afford to have any less street in my business tactics than a bona fide pimp or hustler. I still am part pimp, and I've always been a full-blooded hustler. You take an X-ray of me, it ain't bone that you see—it's asphalt. As in, 100% pure street. It ain't a joke, man, cuz I could fall just as flat as any of these fools if I let myself get soft and lenient. But guess what? There wouldn't be no one like me out here to save my ass, unlike the situation these fools have. Hold up. Take that back. There is One that would save me. My Lord and Savior Jesus Christ. But besides that, no one out here in this particular ecosystem.

The reason for that is that I am an original. An innovator. No one else does what I do. No one else shares the destiny I've carved out for myself.

Still with me? Good. Cuz you about to meet two legends under the management of yours truly: Sonny B with his trumpet, and Old Miss Henry Jameson with her attitude and rotten smell. Got the two of them stationed over at the Burger King as a married couple, though they ain't really married, and hell, not even friends. Temporary setup, I keep reminding Sonny B. Living conditions really getting to him lately, smell really getting to him, plus having to carry the damn stage play like a one man show, Old Miss Henry being a diva who won't memorize her own damn lines. Script has them traveling the Earth as man and wife for like sixty-some odd years now ever since they honeymoon, searching for they kid who was stolen by some UFO muhfuckas. Now that's some inspired bullshit. Inspiring, too, judging from the coin the public's been bringing in this week.

At least, until today. See that cup next to Sonny B? The one between his shoe and that catatonic mess leaning against the wall?—Old Miss Henry, by the way—well, that cup's usually filled with green and silver by now. Seems like some aliens from the script must've come ripped us off or something. Excuse me for a minute. Gotta go look into this.

"Hey Sonny, what's with the empty cup?"

"Damn, P, we been waitin' for you. Why ain't you tell us you double-booked this place today? You tryna start a three-ring circus? Me and Old Miss Henry here already two separate rings ourselves. Don't be needin' no third to help us out."

"What the hell you talkin' about, Sonny? You on that H again? I already got one damn junkie to look after."

"Man, you know I ain't touched that shit in years. Though this here, ahem, *lady*, be makin' my ass think twice. Uh-uh, P. I think you startin' to get too large a roster. Got too many damn clients to keep track of, if you ask me."

"Hold up, Sonny. Let's start over. I think we on a different page or somethin' today."

"Whole world's on a different page if you ask me. Your new client over there's been stealin' our thunder from minute one."

"New client? You mean Lil' Hivvy? Nah, I got him posted up on the boulevard. You know I'd never put his sorry-ass mumble rap up against your fearsome trumpet."

"No, not him. Whoever the guy with the crown is. What he call himself again, Old Miss Henry? King somethin' or other. King Wisdom? No. King somethin'. Anyway. The guy with the crown over there."

"Guy with the crown? I don't have any guy with a crown."

"You sure?"

"Positive. I've never had anyone like that."

"Then maybe you should see for yourself. Could be one of them damn independents I thought we ran out of town. Anyway, he's been drawin' quite a crowd over there all morning. Wipin' us out over here on this side."

"What the fuck? I'mma have to go check this out."

Come on. Follow me. Let's move. Need to see what the fuck's going on.

Well, I'll be damned. Ain't this some shit. You seeing what I'm seeing or what?

You believe this dude? I mean, who the fuck does he think he is?

King Common Sense, apparently. That's who. Judging from the cardboard sign tied around his neck and the Burger King crown on top of his head. And let me guess. That crate must be his throne. *A few cents for my two cents.* Okay. Decent tagline, I'll give him that. Too bad there ain't no such thing as friendly competition. You either with Mistah P or you not. And if you not—like this clown—you'd best stay around your own way.

Look at this fool. Got the nerve to come up into my stronghold, one of my flagship locations, and take the very side of the parking lot opposite Old Miss Henry Jameson and Sonny B. Ain't a secret they under the management of the one and only Mistah P, so no way this fool's oblivious to the meaning of his act. This look like a declaration of war to me. I ain't having it. Plain disrespect.

Here, make yourself useful. Go on over there and see what he has to say.

You. Yes, *you.* Who you *think* I'm talkin' to? Go on

over there and see what he's all about.

Well, go on then. Pretend you just walking by. And don't say you with me. I'll just stand back here and listen in. *Go on!*

Good. Yeah. Now do something to make him start up. Uh-huh. That's it. You got him started. Now let's see what this fool's all about:

"Good afternoon, weary traveler. I'm King Common Sense. A few cents for my two cents, what do you say?"

Psssssst! Don't give him any money!

"Who are you looking at over there? Is that your friend? *What?* Your *tour guide?* What kind of tour are you on?"

Psssssst! Hey! What the fuck you doing? Don't make conversation, just see what his routine's all about!

"Who *is* that over there? Okay then, never mind. Say what? You wanna know what my *routine* is all about? Well honestly, I don't consider myself a performer. Just a man with worldly wisdom. Everyone could use a little piece of wisdom, no? A few cents for my two cents isn't a bad deal, after all. What do you say? Spare some change for a piece of wisdom? A ray of light in the darkness of life?"

Hey! What are you doing? I said don't give him any money!

"Thank you, friend, for your kindness. This is the piece of wisdom I have for you. Cherish the children of the world, for they are the future. All hope and strength lies in their little hands. Now go with God, my friend, for He is our Lord and Protector. And tell your friend over there to come over too if he likes."

That's right. Get your ass back over here. Traitor. How much you give him, anyway? And why you smiling? What, you trying to say you bought that bullshit? I've gotten better fortune cookies at Chinese drive-thrus. Now if you'll excuse me, I have an invitation to accept. *His.* Gonna nip this muhfuckin' cancer in the bud. Here he go starting up already, and I ain't even made it over there to him yet:

"Oh, wonderful. I was hoping you'd come over. Hello, weary traveler. I'm King Common Sense. I saw you standing over there while I was talking to your friend."

"Yeah? And what, you ain't recognize me?"

"*Should* I? "

"The name Mistah P ring any bells?"

"Afraid not."

"Well guess what, fool, I'm the only genuine king around here. And if you had any *real* common sense, you wouldn't have parked your crate anywhere near my territory."

"Sorry?"

"Yeah, you'd *better* be. And you'd *better* get the fuck up out this place."

"No, I meant, *sorry, I have no idea what you're talking about or who you are.*"

"You one ignorant muhfucka then. Must have been newly born into the world, else you'da heard my name round these parts and known this venue is mine. Those two old folks I'm sure you saw on the other side of the parking lot? They mine. In fact, this entire eight block radius? All mine. Any beggar you see in these parts."

"Any but *me*, then."

"Yeah, any but you. *Exactly.* That's why you'd best be leaving these parts unless you interested in my representation."

"*Representation?* Ha! Representation for *what?* I've *got* my act together, as you can see. But you know, that's funny. Cuz you know what it sounds like to *me?* It sounds like you're afraid of a little competition."

"Oh I see, then. I see how it is. You gonna try and call me out like that. Gonna try and disrespect me in front of this here audience I'm showing around. That's fine. I can play like that. I ain't had a challenge in a while. That's what happens when you crush the competition. Ain't no one left to challenge but yourself. Fine, then. You wanna challenge me? I *accept.* I'll show you how I became the king of this here market. Tell you what. Rare opportunity for you. We'll see who earns more by the end of the day. My two people over there or you over here. Whoever lose gotta give up their claim on this place and spread the word."

"Very well. But does the money I already earned today count? Cuz if so, you're starting off at a distinct disadvantage. You may want to think this out."

"I've done thought it out, and yes, the money counts. Every penny you've earned so far against every penny my people haven't, but *will.* And believe me. They *will.* You'll be gone by the end of the day. Believe that."

"I'll believe it when I see it."

"You ain't such a prophet, then."

He's lucky I can just turn around like that and walk away. You believe that muhfucka? Took all my strength not to hit him. He lucky I ain't into violence these days.

Come on. We ain't got much time. I got to come up with something. Got to sit on this here curb and think. Think. Come on, P. *Think.*

You been in this game long enough to handle a fool like this. Don't pretend like you weren't expecting this to happen. You knew it would. Elevate the game, and it eventually elevates itself up to your level. Entrepreneurial escalation or something like that.

It all comes down to this. The point when you gotta prove you the boss for a reason. Because you can't let no one steal your destiny. Not even a piece of it.

Think!

Hold up. Reality check time. Gotta face the situation

we in, bad as it may be. Sonny B is a tired old man. Old Miss Henry Jameson is useless. You just carrying they asses cuz you feel sorry for them and trying to keep them from becoming obsolete. Cuz you want to protect them from the changes you made to the market. The revolutions you brought on by elevating the game the way you did. Making it a service industry instead of a charity. Giving people the expectation of talent and intrigue instead of just some old fool holding out a cup. Let's face it. You failing to live up to your own standards. That tired-ass story you got Sonny B delivering about UFOs stealing he and Old Miss Henry's baby just ain't cutting it no more.

I mean, look at this woman right here. The look on her face as she's trying to go into the Burger King. Looks like she's being pulled in two different directions. Got a baby all up in her arms crying, and here's Sonny B delivering the tall tale that's supposed to be funny in a *wink-wink, you-know-this-ain't-true* sort of way, but the woman ain't even got a smile on her face. She's just standing there in disbelief, starting to twist her face all up into a hateful expression. Look like she's about to go off on poor Sonny, who's giving the story his all, as you can tell by tuning in:

"… but then they lights come shinin' through the bedroom window again, see… and I says to my little old wife Miss Henry here… I says, 'Honey, them alien ships is back! And they fixin' to take away our little Tyrone!'"

And then, watch this, watch Old Miss Henry chime in and turn the whole damn routine to shit. How much you wanna bet that's what she's gonna do:

"I ain't your damn wife," she says. Just like I told you she would.

But then, like the true pro he is, Sonny tries to pick up the pieces and redeem their act:

"Uh… see, them aliens… them aliens ain't just stole

our little Tyrone… nah, see… them extraterrestrials was extra cruel that night… used they tractor beam to steal my little Miss Henry's mind, too."

Nice job, Sonny. Nice try, at least. But now it's for nothing, what with Old Miss Henry chiming back in to take another shit on credibility:

"Ain't nobody steal my damn mind. Won't no damn aliens, neither."

See what I got to put up with? What Sonny got to put up with? Speaking of. Go on now and improvise around her, Sonny. Do your thing:

"See, she crazy ever since. My poor little Miss ain't right no more, ever since them extraterrestrials landed. Stole her mind and our little Tyrone and we been havin' to travel round ever since, roundin' up the proper funds so we can build a ship of our own, see, with lasers and photons and what not… gonna travel up into space so we can rescue our little Tyrone back."

This ain't going well. And Old Miss Henry ain't even done fucking it up yet:

"I ain't never heard of no damn Tyrone."

Time for the plea. It's a miracle this woman with the baby's still even standing here. Hit it, Sonny, before she leaves:

"So anyway, we was wonderin' if you might, like, have some spare change to give up… you know, seein' as how our cause is noble and you look like a nice person and all… I mean, seein' as how you got your own little tyke there and all, we sorta figured as much as you could put yourself in our shoes…"

Get ready. Here comes the woman with the baby's response. Ain't gonna be pretty from the look on her face:

"Ninja, what I look like, the Salvation Army? I gots to watch out for mines, fool. This here little ninja keep my ass runnin' twenty-four seven. Cry all night like a bitch and keep me from sleepin'. Then be wantin' to have his diaper changed like a hunnit times a day cuz he either pissed or shit himself again. Damn. And you talkin' that shit about spaced invaders comin' up into your crib and takin' your little Tyrone from you? Damn, where them spaced invaders at? Where them little green ninjas, fool? Cuz they welcome to pay this here little crib a visit. That's what *I'm* sayin'. Take this here little ninja off my hands for a while, that'd be nice."

Hold up. Clouds starting to part in my head. Little idea starting to shine through. But nah. Nah. Or then again. Maybe. Need a minute to figure this out. Let her ramble on some more while I think:

"… and that mind-stealin' bullshit? Ninja, wouldn't even be a daddy's mind to steal up where I stay. Least your ass got *somebody*, even if it is this here smelly-ass ho."

Old Miss Henry: "I ain't nobody's damn smelly-ass ho."

Woman with baby: "I ask you, bitch? Damn, fools like you make my ass sick. Sittin' all up on they ass all day, waitin' for sympathy and shit. Like the world owes 'em for somethin'. Get your ass up, bitch! Least your husband here do somethin' for his. Play a mean-ass trumpet, I heard his shit before. Been out in my parts since I was just a tyke. But you… look at you… probably been restin' your lazy ass against the side of this building your whole life, waitin' for the world to take a likin' to you when you ain't done shit to make 'em like you for!"

Old Miss Henry: "What you say?"

Oh shit. Old Miss Henry's up on her feet. Never seen that happen before.

Woman with baby: "Sit down, bitch. You ain't deaf. You heard what I said."

Much as I'd like to see the Old Miss get hers, that

little idea of mine is ripe and ready. Time to break this up and let the negotiating begin. Observe:

"Ladies, ladies. Please. I've got a little business proposal I think can clear this up."

Woman with baby: "Who the fuck is you?"

"Name's P, as in the one and only Mistah. But your ass can think of me as the new salvation in your life."

"Say what? Ninja, please. All talkin' like you the Messiah or somethin'."

"Check it… not the Messiah. I ain't go there. Only one Lord and Savior up above. But I do come in search of that Baby Jesus you holdin' in your hands."

"The fuck you talkin' about?"

"What you *think* I'm talkin' about?"

"How the fuck I know unless you say?"

"Well, what you *think* I was gettin' at?"

"What was you *tryin'* to get at, ninja?"

"I'm tryin' to get at that baby up in your hands."

"Ninja, what? What you think? This here baby's for sale or somethin'? You crazy if you think this little ninja's for sale."

"Yo, I ain't say nothing like that."

"Then what, ninja? What you want with this here little tyke?"

"Is he heavy?"

"Say what?"

"*Is he heavy?* I asked if he's heavy. Cuz if he a burden, I can offer to give you a break."

"Speak English, ninja. Talk straight if you think we on the same page."

"What page *you* on?"

"What page *you* on?"

"What book we talkin' about? Cuz if we talkin' the Good Book, then I'm on the page where the Mother Mary leave the Baby Jesus in the care of the Three Wise Men while she go out on the town and get to know Bethlehem again, minus the burden she's been carrying around."

"Just what you proposin', ninja?"

"Nah, see, the question ain't: *What Mistah P proposin'?* The question is: *What service Mistah P givin' away for free?*"

"Spit it out then, ninja! Tired of all your sales pitch bullshit. Just get to the damn point!"

"Fine, then. Look here, sister. What's your name, anyway?"

"Tyaina."

"Look here, Tyaina. You got a babysitter lined up for the afternoon or what?"

"*Babysitter?* Ain't no damn *babysitter* up in my life. Else I wouldn't be carryin' this little ninja around every damn where I go."

"That's what I thought. Well, you in luck today, Tyaina. Cuz you lookin' at your brand new babysitters for the afternoon."

"Babysitters? Hold up. Why you wanna watch this little ninja? Ohhhh. Hold up. Hold up. I get it. You gonna use him as a prop for these two beggin' fools, is that it? So you can try to earn more money and shit."

"I won't lie to you. That's exactly what it is I'm gonna do. But your baby will be safe at all times. You have my word on that."

"Hold up. How I know you ain't gonna steal his ass or sell him off or somethin' before I get back?"

"Cuz look at me. I'm just a businessman trying to get mine and stay right in the eyes of the Lord. Ain't too many can do both on these streets, but me, no, I'm different: I can. And do. And will continue to, long after you have your baby back in your arms, after he done been showered with praise and gifts from the people, and after they all done blessed his name. Speaking of. What's his name, anyway, this little angel you got here—this little angel about to be in my care today?"

"Mofo. Name's Mofo. But don't be gettin' ahead of yourself. I ain't gave you the go-ahead just yet."

"Come on now, Tyaina. You ain't gotta play. Neither one of us got time for that."

"I ain't playin'. The answer's *yes*. But I do got some conditions for you and yours."

"Fine, then. Let's hear them."

"First, this here smelly-ass ho don't get to touch his ass under no circumstances."

"Okay, then. I can deal with that."

(Old Miss Henry: "I ain't wanna touch your damn baby, no how.")

"Secondly, I don't want no stories being told about how this little ninja's the son of some alien muhfuckas or some stupid shit like that."

"Damn! But okay. I'm a man of my word."

"And thirdly, I want his ass back here in exactly four hours. Is that clear? *Four hours.* Now repeat that shit back to me."

"Four hours. Got it. That's all the time I need."

"Fine, then. I'm out. Gonna—how you put it?—see what I've been missin' in Bethlehem. Here you go. This little burden all yours."

"Careful now. Okay sis, got him. Well hey there, little man…"

And *bam*, like that, the transfer is complete. King Common Sense's defeat is secured. If you've learned anything today, then in your own mind, you can already hear the pitch that will bring his false reign to an end, once and for all, in a matter of just a few short hours:

Look here, good sir. This here family is yours. This baby needs food and diapers just like you did. Just like we all did once upon a time.

NATHANIEL BLACKHELM

Back in that time before we learned to do whatever it takes to survive. Before we unlearned that perfect innocence we all started out with. That same perfect innocence that's still right here in the face of this baby boy. Don't it pull at your heartstrings a little, now? Don't it? Don't it make you want to give up some change?

Yes. I will put the baby down into the manger and win. But first, let me look on him a while.

Behold. The key to the future of my empire.

Or should I say: Behold. The future itself.

Kicking and squirming and crying between these hands.

Hands that have pimp-slapped prostitutes.

Hands that have held out a beggar's cup.

Imagine that. The Baby Jesus Hisself between these unworthy hands.

All the promise. All the struggles and profits to come. Life.

Hard to believe. We all start out like this. Like this.

Needy. Helpless. Begging. Whether born onto the streets or not.

Here. You hold him. Hold victory in your hands.

I want to hear what it feels like from you.

The Dark University: Three Nights of a Fall

For E.A.P. at U.Va. back in 1826—your legend endures

Night One: Mid-October, 1997—*Noise*

Father, I feel your presence here tonight. Your face, as it appears beside mother's in the dual, folding picture frame upon my desk, is now my face in the mirror across the room. This family snapshot next to the computer screen is never to be snapped shut; for it is a constant reminder of where I come from: you two, but mostly you. It, like your bearded face upon mine, and the trench coat that hangs next to the mirror—a trench coat I borrowed from your old clothes that last night I was home—is a constant reminder of what I am here to do. That I am to right what happened to you in this lonesome place. That I am here as the reckoning for your fall.

On the application, there was a slot to enter relatives who had previously attended The University. I did well to omit your name. Better they should not remember you. From your fall, they might try to prophesy mine, and then I could push neither of us through: you and I, two halves of the same knife through the gut of this wretched institution that caused a young man's fall more than thirty years ago.

A poor, small town boy with dreams of becoming a doctor had transferred here after two years of community college in his rustic, red dirt region of southern Virginia. He had come here for the prestige of The University's name, the promise of the future it could secure. None in his family had gone to college before him, let alone to such an elite institution—the best in the state, and one of the most renowned universities in the nation. He knew when he walked through the gates that he was entering an exclusive world, though he couldn't have guessed it was one so *exclusionary*. Its curriculum was more difficult than any he had ever faced; its people, unlike any he had ever met. Most, unlike him, were the product of a privileged background and the best private education money could buy. Amidst their masses, he found himself defeated by an overwhelming sense of isolation, alienation, and at the heart of it—inferiority. It didn't help that he lacked the funds for food and other necessities. He ended up failing his pre-med courses and leaving at the end of that first semester here. His dream of becoming a doctor died in this place. Now his son returns a generation later with a score to settle and his own set of dreams.

Mine, father, is a dream of words—an as yet unwritten future in the art of the written word. But no words will come to me in this godforsaken dormitory. The few words on the screen of my desktop PC are blurry; their light, now brighter than the fading autumn sunlight seeping in through the blinds. I've been sitting at this desk all day now with my head in my hands, repeating a familiar prayer:

Make it stop. Please make it stop.

But it is useless after a month and a half. I know by now the noise outside the door will never relent. It reverberates non-stop from the furnished common area connecting this room with the four other double-occupancy rooms of the suite. It is in this common area just outside my door where the suitemates and their friends regularly congregate—their shouting, laughter, music, and endless revelry destroying my concentration at every turn. By the time I wait them out every night to complete my assignments, I can no longer string together a sentence or even hold together a thought. At that hour, I cling desperately to the ambition of what I had wanted to say on the page, but find myself fighting my own mortal limitations, weak as I am with fatigue, beaten into mental desperation by the hours spent awaiting a silence that should be my right but isn't my reality in this maddening House of Chaos and Noise.

As the Sole Worshipper of Silence amongst the Noise-Makers of the Suite, my ears have become attuned to their every little sound—but none more than their whispered mentions of a freakish figure of the night who keeps to himself and can be seen circling the sidewalks and streets in the nightlit hours, like a dog who has lost his way. A figure who doesn't belong here and deserves to be put down. It is the echoes of these whispers I walk into whenever I emerge from my room, crossing through the common area toward the bathroom or front door. So pervasive are the rumors of how deranged I am, how dangerously demented, that even I have begun to have doubts about my sanity—doubts little alleviated by the gradual estrangement of an old and dear friend from back home.

Kiran and I should be brothers here, being two of the few from our southeastern Virginia hometown who made it into this esteemed University. Instead, we have devolved into little more than roommates—his successful integration into University life, a stark contrast to my refusal to socialize and conform. He has his own new friends here, his own new life, while I have rejected any camaraderie with these sons and daughters of the mothers and fathers you, father, must have encountered when you were here. Mothers and fathers who no doubt whispered the same cruel whispers of you.

We are different than them, father, are we not? Different from these alien souls who think more than feel, spout trivial knowledge, score perfection on standardized tests. These remarkably assured people who seem not to have any trace of the same fear that is felt within my heart and worn upon my face at every moment. For them, success here is a given, a legacy. But my legacy is different: it is the memory of the fall you suffered here—a memory I have pieced together from what little you have shared about it over the years. A mention here and there of your walks in the cold from the classes you were failing back to the dormitory—walks of disillusionment and dying dreams. Beyond this recollection, there is the single word you used to describe those few, long ago autumn months: *lonesome*.

But the true testament to how that failed semester affected you—and what it meant in the larger scheme of your life—has remained behind your eyes all these years. It is there in a regret that is detectable in your quietest moments—a deep regret that has haunted you over time: from the time of your first year after leaving here, when you began studying pharmacy at a decidedly less prestigious university, to the time of your second fall, as a middle-aged man.

It's been four years now since that black day in the pharmacy. That fall day in your mid-forties when your colleagues staged an intervention, confronting you with the addiction you had eventually grown careless in concealing. The damning evidence was a shortage in the store's inventory of pills. They were the pills you had been taking ever since pharmacy school—the little white uppers that helped you maximize productivity by boosting your energy and eliminating, whenever necessary, the need for sleep. What the pills could never eliminate was your lingering sense that, as a man who had failed to become a doctor—a man who filled prescriptions for a living instead of writing them—you had somehow ended up a failure in life. But once your colleagues had surrounded you on the day of the intervention, you were lucky to keep what "failed" life you had. Completing an inpatient recovery program was the only way to keep your credentials as a pharmacist. When you returned home after several months, clean, you shaved your beard off as a new beginning—the beard you had worn until the day of your second fall. It is the beard I now wear to commemorate your struggles, and as a sign of our shared fallibility: for I know by now that first fall of yours here— the one that compromised your future—is more likely to be repeated in me than redeemed.

The door flings open, breaking my trance: the thoughts of father that have carried me away in the moments or maybe hours my gaze has been fixed on his face in the left half of the picture frame. Now the noise from the common area rushes in with a vengeance: a spike in the commotion that has plagued me all day, as the sound waves enter nakedly into the room.

"Let there be light!" Kiran flicks the light switch as he enters, flooding the room with blinding fluorescence. The door bangs shut behind him as he tosses his backpack and takes a seat at his computer—another day's studying, all done. If only the library could work for me, too. But its computer labs are in a busy public space on the library's main level. I've tried working there, but the noise, commotion, and limited library hours are no remedy to my dilemma: the dilemma of finding a sustainably peaceful place to work. Surely there is somewhere suited to my needs within the space of this institution. I have to keep believing it exists. Like a shining myth, the prospect lights my thoughts, and has lighted my recent wanderings beyond the dormitory— wanderings I feel a sudden need to continue tonight.

I rise and walk toward my father's reflection in the mirror, taking his trench coat from the hanger and putting it on.

"Going somewhere?" Kiran asks from his computer.

"May as well. I'm not getting anything done *here*." I turn away from him as I pick up the dual-frame portrait and drop it discreetly into the front pocket of my coat.

"Everyone wonders where you go at night."

"Yeah?" I turn back around. "Usually I'm just out doing some crime-fighting."

"Is that the Bat-Cape?" he asks of the flowing black coat.

"Something like that." I head for the door.

"Be careful," he says as I turn the doorknob, opening the floodgates to my tormentors' den. This is the part I hate: trying to pass through the common area with as little interaction as possible, making my hatred known without allowing it to explode from within. I close the door to the room, then move hurriedly past the faces and bodies of the Noise-Makers. They appear as hazy shapes along the couches and chairs: a few of them, suitemates; the others, people I've seen around the circle of neighboring dormitories. All the stupid little boys and girls.

"Going out?" rises a voice above the clamor. The voice of my sworn enemy: Edison. The ringleader of the commotion. It was he who first initiated me into this new world devoid of silence and sleep. That first night here, my first ever prayer for silence—a prayer that originated because of him. To this day, his stereo still thumps through the wall next to my bed during the few hours I try to sleep. Whenever sheer exhaustion wills my knuckles against his door, a smug face answers: Edison, merciless Edison, who knows why I am there, yet still keeps his stereo just loud enough to keep me awake.

I stop and turn to answer the smug face, the face of the institution, surrounded as it is by the other faces of its kind. *Out?* he had asked.

"Better than in," I mumble. I begin to turn the doorknob leading outside.

"Were we too loud?" he asks, an awkward silence descending; his question, meant to mock me in front of an audience. Because he knows by now how meekly I will answer, how certain their dominion over me.

"Uh, no, you're fine." The words complete their path from my mouth. My feet complete their path outside into the cold air of the mid-October night. The night that is a little colder every night. I step out every night and life becomes colder, and I become more afraid and alone. But in that aloneness, no one owns me, and there is a freedom in my wanderings at night. There are moments in my nightlit wanderings when I need but close my eyes and *feel* to know my bearings: I am moving down the sidewalks and streets in long strides, past the streetlights and nightlit fields, with the picture of mother and father in my pocket, and prayers for the future in my heart.

Thinking: Father, too, walked this lonesome path in the cold.

Feeling: His presence with me, here, tonight.

Incanting: *Father, I feel your presence here tonight. Are you not here, father, alongside me?*

An answer brewing in my blood: *Yes.* This too was father's lonesome path in the cold. I can feel it. Feel him within, and all around me, as I walk. Feel that he too crossed this footbridge and saw the lights of the passing cars below. That he—my noble father—was a transient figure here just like me: a young man devoid of any sense of belonging, who would often roam in search of an escape.

His trench coat blows in the wind as I descend a set of stairs to the street below the bridge. As I pass under the bridge, I am startled by a presence: a ragged, homeless man, asleep between the columns of the underpass. To exploit him as a figure of omen is wrong, and yet a relevant exercise in paranoia: for this is my true state of mind. I could fall at any moment. I can and will fall if I do not find a quiet place.

I walk on: my father, my shadow, me.

The three converging in a nightlit field.

My father, my shadow, me.

The three conversing in a nightlit field.

Father appearing to me through the medium of my shadow and speaking to the heart of me. A vision that is a reality that is a nightlit fantastical dream.

"You don't have to do this," he tells me.

"No. I do."

"You're tired."

"I can't work here or get any sleep."

"I have something to help you with that." He extends his hand, a bundle in its grasp: a bundle of nightlit pills in my father's hand. I remember then: father dropping a pocket full of pills in a parking lot, scrambling to pick them up before anybody saw. Asking my help. I did; a boy who helped his father put pills like these back into his inside coat pocket. It was the inside pocket of this very coat; he used to wear it around the time of his second fall.

"With these," he says, now gifting me the pills, "you won't need to sleep anymore. There'll be pockets of silence once you've waited out the noise past the loneliest hours of night."

I take his offering graciously. He winks, then turns to walk away.

"Dad," I say.

He turns back around.

"Thanks."

I let him turn away from me this time, turning my own feet back to walk the way I came: a retread of the sacred path that led me here. One of father's feet that is mine places itself in front of the other before my eyes, moving me forward, taking me back toward the source of all chaos and noise in the world, the place I know I will eventually taste the death of my dreams. Only this night, to accompany me, a new, redemptive discovery upon my person: a mountain full of chalk-white pills in father's coat pocket—the uppers left over from a fallen age.

In the hellplace I am returning to, there can be no sleep. This I have already learned. Yet with the means to purge such a need from my body, I return this night less fallible than before.

Night Two: Mid-November, 1997—*Yearning*

Mother, please hear me. Please help me in the way father cannot: for no chemical exists that could purge this yearning. It is to you, the kindly face in the right half of the picture frame, that I turn for this dilemma of the heart. The moonlight favors you over father tonight, lighting your face, providing the room's only light, that I might discern those parts of me not from him, but you: the depth of my emotions, the breadth of my imaginings, the extent of my loyalty to the man in the left, shadowed frame. To this past month's heartache, I will keep him in the dark; for it is a dilemma better unburdened unto you. For weeks it has been building and festering within, and now culminates in her presence here tonight.

Her voice, mother; do you not hear her voice through the crack in the door? It is the same voice that first spoke to me as I sat on the steps of this dormitory one sunny mid-October afternoon. I had come outside to gather my thoughts as a momentary escape from the noise in the suite. Then a voice sang my name, and she appeared.

"Hey there, remember me? I'm in your writing class. My name is Grace."

I looked up, recognizing her. The girl with the ponytail who sat two chairs away from me in class. The girl I hadn't really noticed before. I asked her if she lived nearby.

"Right up there," she said, pointing one building over, one floor up. "You?"

"Here," I said, gesturing behind me.

"I'm on my way to get some coffee," she said. "Do you want to come?"

I only hesitated slightly, remembering the work I still had left, then unremembering in the instant she smiled.

"I just have to get my purse," she said. I followed her

up the stairs to her suite, waiting in the common area as she got her purse from her room. Then we walked together the path I normally walked alone, crossing the footbridge leading to the outlying areas of the campus. When we reached a row of restaurants and shops, she stopped and opened one of the doors. It was a small but crowded coffee shop. We sat at a table for two, placing our hot drinks in front of us: my hot chocolate to her coffee.

"So where do you come from?" I asked.

"Eden," she answered. Or at least that's how it registered to me. She spoke of the same northern Virginia region I now knew as the place they all came from—a D.C.-adjacent suburbia whose high schools offered college credits to high achievers, enabling its native sons and daughters the chance to enter college with as many as several semesters of academics already fulfilled. I thought of my own region to the south, how it paled in comparison in terms of opportunity. I'd never had anything to compare it with before—its school system, the character of its people.

These days, though, I was being awakened to what appeared to be a new race of man. Intelligent, attractive, affluent: this was their makeup, the result of some type of natural selection I had never known to exist. This was evolution, and it began in an Eden-like place. I pictured it as a place where all the little girls sprouted out of vegetable patches, ripening into perfection. Their beauty was unmistakable, and at all times on display around campus. Yet hers was a beauty that could pass unnoticed, as it had for me in all the time we had shared a class. It was a modest beauty, the kind that most appealed to me—a beauty you could have as only yours. Her long brown hair pulled discreetly into a ponytail. No makeup on her face. A loose shirt that concealed her figure, the shapeliness of which would only become apparent as she would stretch her limbs in her chair.

My God, what was happening? This was normal conversation with another person. This felt good, felt right—felt like *me* for the first time in months. This was sanity: listening to details insane in their inaneness. She told me she liked to sing, and I said I would love to hear sometime. She told me she had worn purple eyeshadow to her prom, to match her purple dress. I said I'd gone alone to mine; that I sometimes tended to do things alone. But I didn't dare tell her how isolated I had become here. I had wanted to seem as normal as I could.

It must have worked. She suggested we have dinner in the cafeteria sometime. Our first *sometime* came the very next day. "Dinner tonight?" she had asked after our long walk home from class. It would soon become a divine routine: class, the walk together back to the dorms, her dinner invitation, then our cafeteria rendezvous later in the evening. There, I would hold her eyes across the table, reveling in her nearness. The confession was becoming harder and harder to stifle. *I have feelings for you, too.* That's all it would have taken to reciprocate her signals to me. Like the way she would always seat us together at the end of some table in the cafeteria, sequestered from everyone else. Or the way she would turn to face me at the midpoint between our two buildings in the heavy, lingering moment before we parted for the night. That was the hardest part—those parting moments. I would want so much to follow her, with more than my eyes, up the stairs, or to have her follow me. I would want so much just to confess to her, in a wordless signal of my own: arms outstretched, inviting the long-awaited complement of her embrace.

And yet I could not—not when there was so much at stake.

A voice had intermingled with hers even the first time she had spoken to me, so that it wasn't just *Hi, my name is Grace,* that I had heard, but *You will fall if you allow this to happen.* It was the voice of fallibility, a voice of extremes. It spoke louder with my every encounter with her, an ugly, unsinging voice of many reminders: I didn't come from where these people did, I didn't have a father who had made it through here like theirs, or a mother who had gone to college like theirs. In short: I didn't have the privilege of being able to waste any time on selfish pursuits. Any time devoted to affairs of the heart would be time away from the righting of father's name—a righting through writing, studying, straining daily to bridge the chasm between my heritage and theirs, the discrepancy between our backgrounds and educations.

And yet, when I felt her slipping, it became too much. I had always known that any of her invitations might be the last, unless reciprocated; that any of our walks together might be the last, unless consummated in some other way. But when the reality of her surrender began, I panicked, not yet ready to become dead in her mind. I willed away the voice long enough to invite *her* to dinner—the first time I had done the inviting. In the cafeteria, I tried to seat us in our usual spot, at the end of some table—but the gesture felt empty, devoid of hope. So did I: the atmosphere was irreparably changed. We ate in silence. She ate fast. I hardly ate. The words never rose. The confession. I could no longer feel it within me. I could no longer feel anything from her.

She walked two paces ahead of me back to the dorms, not hesitating before we parted. She no longer waited for me after class, to walk home. It was over: the promise of what we could have had. Of what I had not allowed to be. And then the aftermath set in, heavy with its solemn rituals. I studied her in class, traversing a barren landscape of nevers with my eyes: all the shapes of her that were now unclaimable by me. And then, at night, I began to study her, too.

Behind the dorms, a steep, tree-lined hill: I had originally set myself upon it in search of refuge, imagining I could dig a hole into it to bury my feelings of regret. What I found instead was a startling vantage point. From this perspective, I could see without being seen, a black shape upon the dark of the hill. The windows to the rooms were lit starkly against the night, my cold breath the only thing endangering my discovery. I controlled it, breathing shallow, pretending myself an unbreathing entity: an anonymous extension of the hillside, a shadowed plant upon its sheltering slope. My feet planted themselves in, my head pivoting across the windows—there was mine, darkened, the ground-level window still cracked from where I had exited. Then one building over, one floor up, was a lighted room, a soft shape moving within. *Her.* For a moment I froze with the thought that she could she see me—but she had moved past the window without any pause. My breath brewed faster, anticipating her return. Moments later, she reappeared, lowering herself to take a seat at her computer, where she would remain for the next hour or so as my limbs grew numb from their static position in the cold. In subsequent nights, I would return to the secret vigil, staring in wonder at the blurred shape of her, wondering what the blurred shape of me would appear as, to her shape above, were I visible: surely a figure more deranged than she had originally perceived. A figure whose way of life here she could never understand.

The same fear is not there in her: the fear of falling that enabled my miracle of will—the withholding of the confession in my heart. To understand that choice and the fear behind it is to understand a life with far more to lose here than hers. So it is that when I sit on the hillside, watching the light from her window and any possible movement she could make, I sometimes see her not as a

NATHANIEL BLACKHELM

beautiful shape in silhouette behind the glass, but a piece of glass with see-through insides. Something hollow, like the rest of her peers. And at the reminder that her path, like theirs, is less fallible than mine, I am provided a moment's relief from her charms.

Still, I cannot release myself from her image. I cannot release myself from the ritual of following her shape in the light. From a dark place of yearning, I have remained embedded, a static, mourning shape on the hillside. There have been no nightlit wanderings of late, no transience beyond my escapes behind the building. I am bound to her image, in the window and within my mind; can neither release myself from it, nor to it. I am unable to force any carnal release to the thought of her. The reminder is simply too painful of what can never be mine.

Tonight, I am faced with the most intimate reminder of all.

She is here. She waits in the common area of the suite. She has come to deliver me a message: this stranger beside her will get to have her tonight. He is a friend of Edison from the suite next door—some guy she has cozied up to lately. They have come by to see Edison before going out for the night. I can see the three of them through the crack in my door: Edison, the stranger, her. The two males converse while she waits near the entrance, perhaps sensing my presence in this room. It is a room whose threshold she crossed only once, leading to the only time our bodies ever touched.

She had waited in my doorway as I rummaged through the drawer of my desk. I searched to fulfill a promise I'd made to her at dinner that night—that I had something to help her stay awake. She needed to stay up late to finish an assignment, and had already stayed up late the night before. I'd wanted to trace the dark circles around her eyes with my fingers, telling her this is exactly how I had pictured the purple eye shadow she'd worn at her prom. But this was not Eden, her world and theirs. This was mine: a space of intense repression. I felt her presence within my room, and something ached. I'd wanted to search the drawer forever, knowing that once I'd turned around and handed her the pill, there would be no further cause for her to stay.

In truth, the search was feigned, the entire scenario, a setup: I had pretended no pills on my person at dinner that I might lure her momentarily into the room. Once there, and finally turning from the drawer of the desk, I had awaited her outstretched hand, delighting in the prospect, the near-guarantee, of a single, unfettered touch. It was a touch that lingered only in my mind; witnessed, it was a mere formality. Yet anticipated, experienced, and instantly mythologized, the touch became a world of its own. It was a place of life, flourishing with promise: the eternal in a flash, then a dead planet of exaggerated remembrance. A touch now parodied in the jarring sight of her hand so visibly, so easily, in the hand of someone else.

She holds it tentatively, as if only half-willing to be here—as if only the half-willing bait in Edison's trap. He must have known I had feelings for her, having seen her the one time she was here before. How ecstatic he must have been on learning his friend was taking her out tonight. He decided to have fun with it, making sure the friend would invite her by, even prefacing her arrival with a lewd conversation outside my door. It was he and the friend singing the praises of her body—then heralding the friend's chances of getting into it tonight. An obnoxious prologue prepared just for me. Now that she's here, their First Act is underway, to be continued in the recesses of my mind… in the acts this stranger will perform on her. The acts she will perform on him. The acts she and I never will.

Relent.

I break the fourth wall and head for the bathroom, ignoring the players, and her gaze that must be fixed on me as I pass. In the bathroom, a bearded face awaits me in the mirror—a face whose resemblance to my father's I almost curse. *Almost.* But then I remember his legacy that I am here to redeem—and the ambition of my own dream of words.

End intermission: I open the door again to find the three of them gone. That's when it hits me—the place hits me with the one thing it has never hit me with before. Silence. The beautiful silence I have craved for months, the quiet I had forgotten could exist in an enclosed space. I start to laugh, arms outstretched, envisioning the usual shapes in the common area: Edison and all the others, the ghosts of their figures, the spirit of their chaos in the air. *Fuck you! And you! And you!* I laugh, my feet twirling around their stationary shapes. It is a wild and angry dance of bitterness and hatred, yet with movements surprisingly full of—of—

Grace.

At the word, the dance ends. I return to my room and shut the door, letting regret pull me down onto the bed. I close my eyes, only to find that a ghost has escaped from the common area into the room: hers. She lays herself down upon me, a terrible weight: memory, fantasy, her image projected forward into scenes that will never take place. She is here, her face next to mine, my everything within hers, as she envelops me. And I know then the reason for the ungodly silence: it is to taunt me with the quiet place she would have been.

It comes fast: the release to her image, but not in any way that I had planned. From behind the eyes, the rumblings of something cathartic. It builds until it bursts, giving way to a spasm of tears. Then the doorknob turns and Kiran barges into the room.

"Anybody in the Batcave?" He flicks on the light as I scramble to wipe my eyes. "Oh, sorry," he clearly notices. "Just gonna head to the bathroom for a sec." He steps out, allowing me a moment's dignity... which is all the time I need to make an escape.

I throw on the coat and ready the window, hurdling one leg over the sill, then the other. My feet touch down outside just as Kiran's silhouette re-enters the room. He pauses at his computer, picking up the slip of paper I've left on his keyboard—the one I leave there from time to time that reads: *Bat-Signal was calling. Don't wait up.* I begin my dash alongside the building, crossing over to the hillside behind the dorms.

The light in her room is out. I do not allow myself to look too long, discerning shapes that may be moving in shadows; would rather pretend myself the only shape amongst the shadows tonight. The power to keep moving is mine, and I wield it, breaking away from the hillside: no longer an embedded plant upon its slope, but an animal on the mend and on the move.

And my path, once more, becomes familiar: the path of my father, in the mid-November night. My footsteps become his, adapted: I run, blurring the lights of the cars passing below as I ascend the steps of the familiar footbridge. On the bridge, a shape of two figures approaches. A man and a woman, hand in hand.

I recognize them, and my stomach drops.

She and the stranger. On their way back from wherever they have gone. Fumbling toward me along the bridge, headed back toward the darkness of her room.

This is how she sees me: hilariously isolated. Deranged, and dangerously alone. And how I see her: beautiful, but a little girl. A little boy's hand held in hers.

I look back at them after they've passed. They are

one shape now, instead of two. They recede down the stairs and out of sight.

I take the steps leading down to the street. The sidewalk is moonlit. I set my moonlit feet upon it, following the light. Mother's light. Mother: the moonlit, right half of the picture frame. Mother: the moon herself, arisen to guide my path. To sing it in the radiant bath of her moonlight. To singe my insides with her moonlit song.

Sing to me, mother, the songs that she will not. For she will not become a part of our line.

Sing to me, mother, a song of your grace. For what you are full of is her name.

Mother to save me from the heartache of her name.

Mother to convince me I was wise.

Mother with her lunatic light to guide her son.

Mother with her moonlit song.

Sing to me, mother, your moonlit song. I am calling on your deliverance tonight.

It is there in the distance, in the distant wailing. It is there, in the distant sound of the train. Mysterious. Soothing. I would hear it from my bedroom window as a child. Somewhere on the horizon, a moving behemoth. An almost unimaginable shape. *No monsters when the train was coming,* you once told me. *Because the train was carrying all the monsters away.* Little myths like that, you could make up on the spot to put my childish fears at ease. A humble, small town woman's lasting gift to her son: the astounding power of imagination. The belief that through the channeling of imagination through words, there was no path too dark to be traversed.

That belief, configuring your moonlight tonight.

I will follow it wherever it leads.

That belief, leading me through the nightlit field where I met father, only farther: past the tree line, through the dirt path. Granting me extraordinary passage.

That belief, blessing me with the light to find these tracks: tracks I thought to exist only in myth. I stand between them for a moment, making certain they are real; then stand off of them, waiting, waiting. For what, I know and yet don't; can imagine and yet cannot. The awe is real. The growing anticipation. The rumbling of the ground. And the wailing. The wailing. It is no longer mine; no longer just there in my head. And the light. The light is no longer that of the moon. It is that of a star, ambling toward me—some magnificent, celestial machine.

I step back from the tracks, preparing for its arrival. It is close now—the wailing, the light. Both are real, and I am there in both: my wailing in the wailing, my shape and the path of the tracks in the light. And the path of the tracks is what I know my path to be: the path from myth to reality, from a place of dreamed imaginings to a place of material existence—ideas of the mind made written, made real. And the behemoth is in a shape as of me: its metal, a mortal covering like my own—one just as susceptible to the communion of touch. I stretch my hand toward the train, toward the cyclone blowing past me, its breath between my fingers, through my hair, billowing father's coat: the breath of God, the breath of all creation and life. Its breath is magnificent, it is a magnificent machine. And as I see my hand outstretched before it, I imagine I have willed it to life: I am its creator, it began as a thought in my head. I turned the behemoth to words and made it real. I could touch it, stretch my hand farther toward it—but I need not. For it is but an extension of me. An invincible appendage. An immortal projection of all that I have lived and seen.

And behind it, in the dark, after the last train car has passed, lie the remnants of what I have forsaken to achieve it: a cadaver on the tracks, a rotted mortal coil, a loose and ruined suit of female skin. Not real, but an effigy—of her body and all its raptures, forever lost. It is the flesh that is the price of my dream of words, the carnal fulfillment I have sacrificed for its future. Mother's light shines upon it, a single, radiant beam. I turn away from the illusion, horrified, relieved. I stumble, then right myself. The weight of me is changed. Lessened. The burden, lessened. Yet the whole of me is more than before. I begin back the way I came, a lightened figure, a figure enlightened in the magical beams of the moon.

Night Three: Mid-December, 1997—*Atrocity*

Yes. I can see it. It begins like this. The atrocity begins like this.

A pillow held in the grip of my hands: the only white in the dark of his room. His sleeping shape, breathing peacefully in the dawn. My own solemn shape there to prolong the sleep. The pillow in my grasp, over his face. My fist, bashing the pillow. Again. Again. Again. The muffled screams. My fist indenting the screams. Then my weight on top of the pillow, to smother him. Pressing down. Releasing the fury. All of it. Yes. All of it. The animosity, made atrocity at last. And then: silence. A silence of my own orchestration. Of my own creation. A quiet place within the demise of him. Unsilenceable Edison, silenced at last. *Oh Christ, what have I done?*

Ka-crack! Snapped back by the sound. His neck, breaking beneath the pillow. Or maybe not: someone breaking a rack instead. The first, violent shot in a game of pool—that deafening crack just now from beyond the door. And then, just after it, the sound of Edison's voice—so that the murder could not have been real. What else have I dreamed, then? My own image, in the mirror across the room? No. This is reality. I am certain. Only… no way to tell how long it has lapsed. I hate it when this happens: the blurring of time and space. Always does, when the pills are starting to wear off.

Door is cracked. Was it closed before? The sound of clacking billiard balls from the common area seeping through…

Clack! Clack! A memory. The same sound at the pool hall back home. Kiran and I, playing pool every Friday night at the dive of a pool hall along the boulevard of our hometown. A pact forged between us, over the clacking: *If we make it into The University, we'll watch each other's backs.* How far we've regressed since then. Kiran's voice is now audible, intermingled with Edison's. A playful camaraderie between them as they shoot around at pool. This must be the sound of their daily match, in the pool hall the common area has become.

Who but Edison, Unsilenceable Edison, to ring in a new era of noise in the Chaos House through his plot to bring a pool table into the suite? And why not, when even Kiran—newly traitorous Kiran—had a hand in making it happen? It was his hand I witnessed drop a bill into the suitemates' collection, then join the sea of other hands in carrying the pool table through the front door last week. He owns a share then, gladly, in this new pandemonium—the usual crowds in the common area, having grown into swarming hordes.

No hordes tonight, though, from what I can hear—from what I can see, too, peering through the crack in the door. Outside it's just the two of them. Edison and Kiran. Some kind of wires sticking out from their heads. Or maybe I'm just seeing things. A sure sign that it's time to refuel. Grab the coat, head to the bathroom, wash down a dose, and I'll be fine: I'll be able to see clearly again.

I push out, stopping their conversation dead in its tracks. *So sorry to interrupt, guys. Don't mind me.* They turn to one another, as if communicating in the wordless way of old friends. So sickening how close they've become.

In the bathroom, I splash some water on my face to clear my vision. Then the door opens, and the two of them step in. They stand there, peripheral shapes in the doorway. I look up, water running down my face. "Can I help you?"

No answer. The same disarming look on both their faces. Stoic. Unfriendly. Strangely coordinated. Now they're trespassing, as far as I'm concerned.

"What's going on?" I ask.

"What's going on with *you*?" counters Edison. Something funny in his voice. Challenging me. To what? *If only you knew what I've just dreamed.*

"Nothing. Why do you ask?"

Silence. The two of them just looking at one another, knowingly. And then I suddenly have a sick feeling what this is all about. The cracked door of my room. The uncharacteristically empty common area. The two of them, now accosting me. I reach into my pocket: the pocket with the pills. An empty pocket. They are no longer there.

"Looking for something?" Edison asks.

"Please tell me you didn't take something from me."

"You're strung out," says Kiran. "You don't need that shit."

"Don't do this. Just give back whatever it is you took."

"If you mean those little pills," says Edison, "they're already long gone. We flushed them while you were asleep."

Asleep? Was I?

"No," I say, my hand covering my mouth. *Oh no no no no no.* Reality, setting in. Chaos and ruin and downfall. I never thought it would come like this. "You've ruined me. Those pills are all I have." The miracles sustaining my consciousness in a body deadened from lack of sleep. The salvation in father's coat pocket, now flushed away.

"We're doing this for *you*," says Kiran. "It's for the best."

"You have no idea what you've done." A new wave rising within me. Anger. Pure indignation. "No. You know what? You *knew*. You *knew* this would ruin me. That's *exactly* why you did it." *And now, of all times. Now, right at the end of the semester.*

"I did this to help you," says Kiran. "It's better than

having your parents find out."

"Don't you *dare* mention my parents." My hands, balling into fists I can barely contain.

"Careful," says Edison.

"You shut up," I point my finger at him. "Stay the fuck out of this."

"He's just here to help," says Kiran. The look of genuine concern in his eyes, at odds with Edison's patronizing smile.

"The fuck he is." I take a step toward the door. Their shapes block my path—just as they did my father. Convening around him, covering his path from all sides: his colleagues, that black day in the pharmacy. The day of his second fall, four years ago. A day they left him defenseless, without escape, forcing a confession: the habit, how long it had endured, from how many stores he had taken the pills. And then he was to be taken away to a rehab facility.

"It'll be rough for a little while," says Kiran. "I've read about it. But you can wait it out in our room until it passes." Oh Jesus. Withdrawal. I'm going to have to withdraw from the institution. The withdrawal from the pills will keep me from finishing the semester. I won't be able to function in those days or maybe weeks. Only one choice, then. Unbelievable.

"Now I have to leave this place, tonight."

"What do you mean?" asks Kiran. "You'll be fine once you've waited it out." *Fine? Has he ever seen someone in withdrawal?* For father, it took weeks—weeks in which he paced the halls of the detox facility, wide-eyed, oblivious, bouncing like a proton from addict to addict, speaking nonsense when he had always been a pillar of silent wisdom. I will not let them see *me* that fallible. I will not endure that humiliation *here*.

"I'm leaving now. Don't try to stop me."

"Let him go," says Edison. "If that's what he wants."

That's right, Edison. Since that's exactly what you'd wanted out of this.

"But…" starts Kiran.

"Move," I insist.

The two of them step back, unblocking the bathroom doorway. I brush past them into the common area, hearing their footsteps behind me as I reach the front door.

"You don't have to do this," says Kiran. *Neither did you.*

"Don't worry, he'll be back," scoffs Edison.

I turn around, glaring at him. The atrocity from my dream in my gaze. *For your own sake, you'd better hope not.* I right myself, hurtling forward through the exit, emerging the other side a transient entity. Evicted now. Hopeless. Yet I know what to expect: a world where all reality has fallen through. The world of my father, during the time of his second fall. A time when he would see all manner of things. An entire universe, hallucinated within his cell in the detox facility. Imaginary bugs, crawling along the walls of his room. He would reach into the air and close his hand around something. Then open it: nothing there.

"What do you see?" mother asked him the first time we visited.

"Spiders," he said.

"Show me where," she requested.

He pointed to the floor, guiding his finger in a path along the walls and up to the ceiling.

"Everywhere," he said, reaching out again at nothing, closing his hand around it, drawing it in. I burst into laughter. Mother's look of reproach gave way to a smile. My stomach started to hurt from laughing so hard. I couldn't help it. There was a hilarity in the absurdity of father's pantomime—a strange comedy in the exhibition of his plight.

It is a plight now mine; the laughter, soon to become that of the institution. No telling what manner of spiders I will see. I will no longer be able to trust my own eyes. I set them before me, already disbelieving. The drones cannot be real. The circle of dormitories—the slope leading down from each building in the circle—suddenly teeming with nightmarish shapes. An army of drones, descending the hill from every side. Surrounding the figure at the center of the grassy field below. The lights, turning on in the surrounding buildings. The inhabitants, emerging onto the railed walkways of each floor to watch the lone figure's imminent demise at the hands of the drones.

The figure spreads his arms, perhaps surrendering, perhaps welcoming them. Either way, he succumbs to their multitudes. They eradicate him from all sides, reaching into the heart of him, pulling out all hopes for his future. Extinguishing his extraordinary light. Then they leave him a husk upon its back: a nothing figure to be swept away in the mid-December rain—the drizzling rain that is his mother's tears. For in her guise as the moon, she weeps for him, weeps for what they have done to him, and for what he will now never be able to do: complete his studies here, earning noble passage through the exit gates of the institution. Instead, he is to be purged prematurely, human bile to be carried along a river of lunar tears. Carried back to the dead end town where he began, and will now, inevitably, end.

I recognize myself as the figure in the field. And yet I recognize a different path in my feet: the path of my father, traversed so many times before, that takes me back to where he had first offered me the salvation of the pills. Over the footbridge. Down the stairway. A shadowed figure making his way along the street. Alone, as always. As alone as the solitary fields. One particular field amongst them, no longer solitary.

A shape in the field. The shape of me. My father, in the shape of a young man. The young man he was when he was here. A man in rags. Frenetic. Wild-eyed. Like the figure he would become in the detox facility.

"*Father*?" I ask. The word alien, somehow. Because there's no way it can possibly fit the youthful figure before me.

"Not yet," he answers. "But for now, a very dear friend."

"Did you bring more pills for me?"

"No. Not pills. Something even better."

He reaches into his tattered jacket and pulls out a folded sheet of paper. I reach across time and take it from his grasp.

"What is it?" I ask, unfolding the page.

Upon the hand-drawn map is a horizontal line. Above the line, the word *ABOVE*, with nothing else written. Below it, the word *BELOW*, with a winding line ending at a starred-off point near the bottom right corner of the page.

"You've heard of the underground tunnels," he says.

"You mean the steam tunnels?"

He nods. "They run the length of the campus."

"I've seen the grates here and there. The steam rising from them. I've seen the first few rungs of a ladder below the grates."

"Climb down and follow the tunnels to the starred-off point on the map. That's where you'll find it. A single wick. A fuse. All you have to do is light it."

He tosses me something. I catch it. A book of matches.

"What happens when I light it?" I ask.

"The whole place goes up in flames."

"I can see it," I say, imagining the devastation. "But why me? Why not you?"

"Because I already had my chance. This is yours. For both of us. For all the others, too."

"Others?"

"Did you think you were only doing this for you and me?"

He turns around and walks the other way, leaving the nightlit field solitary again. I push on, following the map. No longer any hesitation within me. I am pure kinetic energy, certain of my path. Not running away this time. Running *toward*. For once, on the offensive. The means to wreaking havoc, held firmly within my hands.

Here is the point of entry: one of the many grates I have stepped over before, peering down into its teethed mouth, wondering what world I would be swallowed into were I to descend. I look around: the coast is clear. I wrap my hands around the bars of the grate and pull, dislodging the portal to the world beneath.

Below, the rungs of the ladder are dimly lit. My hands and feet alternate rung by rung, forging a motion of controlled descent. The heat is already stifling. The steam ascends past my face and moving limbs. I touch down upon the grated flooring, peering up through the portal I have traversed. High above me, through the rising swirls of steam, the moon is visible. *Mother. Do not see me here. Do not look upon your wayward son, tonight.*

I advance along the grating. Small track lights line the tunnel on either side. I push on unchallenged toward the starred-off point on the map. And here I was, imagining a more treacherous path. I round a corner, finding myself within a blackened chamber, its walls lined with a set of hollowed columns. And in these columns—or rather, encasements—I see housed the shapes from my vision. Each coffin-like encasement houses the body of one of the nightmarish drones.

The bodies are perfect. Naked. Some male, some female. Standing ramrod-straight in the open-faced metallic husks. Small wires run into the craniums. IVs to the brain. This is the preparation. Everything the drones will ever need to know. All of it. The guarded knowledge. The exclusive traditions. The means to finding connections. The blood-delineated legacies of privilege that will guide their daylit paths in the larger world. All of it is there for them from the start, and I am here to witness their beginning. Here to witness how it is that they are born superior to me.

It is not enlightening. It is enraging. I think of burning them with the matches, but then think better of it—for I am here to wreak more havoc than that. I look to my map. The fuse should be just up ahead. Yet a door father hadn't indicated stands in the way. I turn the handle, surprised to find it unlocked.

Oh Christ, no. Father… what have you done?

Father in a darkened room, hanging from a noose. The chair he has kicked out from under him, toppled onto the floor.

Father slumped in a chair, a bullet through his head. The spent gun dangling from his finger.

Father in a straitjacket, a spilled pill bottle beneath him. His lifeless mouth overflowing with bile and foam.

A trio of effigies speaking to father's nature. Like some kind of grotesque museum exhibit. Its message: that his falls were self-inflicted—the fault of no one but himself. The fault of no *place* but within himself. The institution's side of the story: any failures were by no hand but his own. And all at once, my mission is for nothing. The mirage, like some kind of underground security system, has served its purpose. Disarming me. Disheartening me. Successfully deterring me from pushing forward to light the fuse. For while I know the grim scenes defy reality—father lives and breathes as surely as I do—some part of me fears there is truth in their characterization of his trials.

That noise. Something stirring behind me…

The drones. They're coming awake.

I double back past the drones emerging from their encasements, running: away again, no longer toward. I've failed to wreak the havoc I had hoped. I leap up and catch the rungs of the ladder, climbing up to ground level and pulling myself to my feet. There is no time to readjust the grate. Futile, anyway, to even try. There is no stopping them now. They're coming for me. The only question that remains is—no, not even a question—

More an inevitability I can feel within.

Edison. Unsilenceable Edison. The source of all noise and chaos in the world. If I can't bring an end to the institution, I will settle for an ending to *you*.

There it is. The hillside. The circle of dormitories situated upon it. And there, locked in my sights, the infamous Chaos House.

House of Celebration, where the party never stops.

House of Desecration, where noise kills dreams.

All sources of noise will be destroyed by my hands. By God and my father, they will.

All sources of noise, encapsulated in one. I needn't say his name anymore.

No one stirring anywhere: not out on the railed walkways, not in the windows of the suites. Soon, they will all have cause to emerge.

I descend the walkway to the Chaos House. I open the front door and enter. All is quiet. All is still. I walk past the pool table and open the door to my room. There lies Kiran, asleep. *He meant well; I will hold him in no contempt.* I walk over to my bed. The darkness is thick. The white pillow shines out like a beacon. I take it in my grasp—in one hand, then both. Then I walk back through the darkness of the room. Shutting the door gently as I exit. Turning to look beside me. At *his* door. I needn't say his name.

I close the space between his door and mine. My hands, trembling against the pillow.

Knock. Knock. Knock. Three knocks, just like the first time I ever asked him to turn down his stereo. A request denied a thousand times over. He offered me no mercy. *Remember that.*

My hands do, gripping the pillow tightly. Thinking: *We can do this. We can do this. We can do this atrocious thing.*

The door cracks open. Edison, disheveled from sleep. The pillow, still gripped tightly in my hands.

"What is it?" he asks groggily.

"I…"

Something behind me. A gathering presence. I turn around to see the drones descending the hill.

"I forgive you," come the words from my mouth. I hear their echo before I realize what I have said. Before I know why it must be true. He is nothing to me. A no one. The mere scapegoat for a larger truth: I have never belonged here. I never will.

I turn away from his bewildered face, dropping the pillow. I open the front door and re-emerge into the night— into the light of the approaching dawn. The moon is high and bright above me. *Mother. You can look now. You can start to shed your tears. Can't you see? They're finally coming to send me home.*

I descend the steps of the Chaos House. There are hundreds of the drones, approaching slowly from all sides. I walk forward into the grass. I walk until I am at the center of the grassy field, encircled by the dormitories, and the approach of the relentless drones. The lights come on in the dormitories, one by one. One by one, the inhabitants emerge onto the walkways of their respective floors, crowding the railings to watch the approaching drones extinguish my light.

In they come. Close now. So close. My arms, extending as if by instinct. The figure in the vision from earlier tonight: it was surrender and welcome at once. *Come, then. Come on. I will offer no resistance. I know I don't belong in this place.*

I close my eyes. I feel them seize me. A thousand arms from a thousand different sides. Pulling me apart, piece by piece. Gene by gene. Then I feel the first drops of rain. Mother's tears. A sizzling sound upon me as they fall.

I smell something burning in the dawn. I hear the sound of crumpling leaves.

Then I open my eyes to an incredible sight.

The drones are crumpled leaves on the ground.

My shoulders are smoking in the dawn-lit rain.

Father's coat is seared from the flames that must have protected me. The flames that must have emerged from within.

I was captured, but they were not able to hold me. Against my skin, their feeble hands turned to dust.

They were not able to purge me from this place. It will take a lot more than what they have.

For I am more than one: I am at least two. Myself, and my father before me.

I am at least two, and many more yet—among them, the "others" my father alluded to.

I am anyone who never made it into the gates of this University.

I am anyone who made it in, but not all the way through. Perhaps they left without finishing because their backgrounds had failed them; or refused to assimilate, but found the isolation too much to bear.

I am the life they led after falling here. I am the desolate towns to which they returned, the desolate livelihoods they were left to settle for.

I am the sickness of their bitterness and regret. A sickness that became an insanity in time.

I am that sickness, that insanity.

I am the virus of their multitudes, unleashed upon the singularities so long at rule in this place. I am a devastating plague of human difference.

I am an army.

I am a revolution.

I am the unmaking of this ancient world: column by column, pillar by pillar, effigy by ancient effigy. I will crumble the statues of these sons' and daughters' fathers, and erect new statues of my father in their place.

I will lead my army of the fallible, my fallen father beside me, and topple this kingdom of inherited favor. I will expose it in the tablets of history for what it is: the monarchy beneath the guise of meritocracy. The blood-delineated legacies that fuel it, and that it, in turn, continues fueling in the larger world. The fundamentally exclusionary way of life those lineages adopt.

I am here to herald the proclamation: *We will not be excluded anymore.*

By God and my father, I have seen the years pass. If years is all it takes, then I will endure.

Insane. Have I gone insane, thinking like this? How can I even think like this, if I don't know where I am?

A figure at dawn, lying in a rain-soaked field—the rain-soaked field in front of the dorms. This is where I must have collapsed after the intervention. Only… what part after that was real? Father? The tunnels? The averted atrocity upon Edison? The rise and fall of the nightmarish drones? I know not, and can surmise only this: father's drug is finally purged from my system. I can feel it. The withdrawal and its delusions are complete.

This is reality. I am certain. Certain that I am standing, where I had fallen down before. Certain that I have remained in the place I was prepared to leave—the place I will remain until I prevail. Here. Not home. By God, never home again. Not until it's finished, once and for all…

Or until it finally finishes *me*.

And it hasn't. Not yet. I'm not finished yet.

By God and my father, I'm not finished yet.

A Consecrating Rain

A quarter till midnight.

The last night of summer.

Our two bodies lying together... in a lie. A false configuration of togetherness.

So quiet in here, I can hear the mist outside. The death of summer is heavy in the air.

Here lies the conquest, his limbs thrown over mine. If I move, he will awaken, along with my obligation to sleep here tonight. Already tonight we have slept with each other, giving his body a ghostlike quality. But I have not allowed myself to fall asleep.

There is darkness and weight and change all around us. As he sleeps, he may be seeing it in his dreams. I have my own waking dreams staring up at the ceiling, trying to figure out how we ended up like this. How I ended up staying over, when I should have been long gone by now. How I let myself utter the promise to sleep here till morning.

God only knows. Or maybe the god*s*, plural. The ones I can feel looking down on me with scorn. As if someone has been murdered, their blood scattered about the room. But that is not the case. So why should this feeling of regret stab my conscience? I made no false promises, beyond that of staying the night. Then again, it doesn't matter what words I said. They were in one language; the actions of our bodies, in another. I must still be held accountable for my lust. The gods do not let me off easily. They paint a picture of exactly what they see.

Two new lovers lie in bed together.
One man is awake, but the other is not.
There is nothing between them save the sheets.

I see the fact of us from the ceiling. That there is no 'us' and never will be. Neither the commodity of time nor the intention of longevity is anywhere to be found in the room. We are lying in the bed in a lie. A lie against the soul and all its promise. The life beyond this empty portrait of limbs. We have no future together. We barely even have a past.

Fatigue starts to overtake me, the lay of his limbs still victorious over mine. His body still pinning mine to the bed as he sleeps, enforcing the promise I made to stay here tonight. Why shouldn't I give in, allowing myself to sleep? An answer flashes in my mind, lighting the room. It is a reminder: I have never shared sleep with anyone before. Those I've slept *with*, I have never slept *beside*. It is a gift I shouldn't waste here tonight. So it is that I must stay awake. I must rely on the sound of the mist to sustain me. Even now, it beckons me from outside.

Come, it says. *You must leave before the summer sleeps.*
"But I can't leave without waking him," I say.
Yet if you stay, nothing good can become of it.
"Then what am I to do?"
Pay heed to the time. Midnight is upon us.
A solution presents itself as we speak.

This must be deliverance: in the freeing of my limbs from their binding entanglement… in my regained ability to move about the room. I lift up the window, preparing the passageway to the front yard. My head breaches the opening like a crowning infant. Then it all rushes in—the mist and night air, the glow of the streetlights and all the radiance of a brand new season awaiting me outside. My lower half emerges, completing the delivery. As I stand, the night air

NATHANIEL BLACKHELM

swirls around my brain.

A flash like lightning. The flash: a bolt of memory. His body, breathing heavily. Then its weight was no longer on top of mine. But how did he manage to sleep through my escape? The gods chime in, describing what they see back inside.

Summer has ended.
A man lies in bed alone.
He will never awaken again.

I look at my hands, holding them out before me. They are bloody. Yet I am not bleeding. Another lightning flash: of memory. The moments just after midnight, surging back into my mind. The apple slices on the plate by the bed. The paring knife beside the plate. The deft move that had freed me from his limbs: I had reached for the knife with my free hand, stabbing through his neck.

I fall to my knees. I was here at the turning of midnight. I was here for the turning of the season, at summer's end. I was still in the room when the turning overcame me: when this familiar, murderous part of me succumbed, as it always has, to the onset of fall. Now his body sleeps forever—the first of the year to lie lifeless because of me. The first ever of my quarry not a stranger, but someone more: a soul known to me intimately before the deathblow.

Heavy now. So heavy. There can be no deliverance from this.

Then a miracle from above: a lightness, beginning to sprinkle itself onto my shoulders. It is the mist, having congealed into the first autumn rain. Transformed from its former state. Fully realized, and awash upon my limbs. Not washing away the red so much as consecrating it. Making it sacred, like the yet preserved gift of a first shared sleep.

Deus Rx Machina

Below me, so far below me, the junkie lies in wait: the way I first found him, the way I find him every night. Kneeling. Wailing. Praying for me to come with his fix. The smell of his feces wafts up as I descend onto his rooftop from the building above. He sits in his usual place on the little gravel rocks, wallowing in squalor, a pool of urine puddled beneath him, the usual shit pile gathered behind his ruined pants.

"You shit yourself again," I say.

"Man of the rooftops! Where the fuck you been all night?"

"Really, man of the dregs—is that any way to greet your king?"

He looks like a prisoner, walled in by the waist-level barriers that line the apartment building's rooftop. I let him ramble on in his favorite way.

"Fucking shit-for-brains man of the rooftops, always gotta be making me wait. I didn't miss you that much, anyway," he lies.

"Shit-for-pants minion, I do love it when you play hard to get."

Out comes my briefcase from the drape of my coat. I slowly unlock the latches.

"You got nothing," he says. "You got nothing that can fill me up."

"Holes for your holes. That is all I've ever had for you, Darrian."

I open the briefcase to show him my line. He eyes my serums like the madman I have made him. He reaches up from his shit-stained life for the one that has been primed just for him.

"Just for you," I say, handing him the needle.

He accepts it with delight, knowing the time is close now—the time to which the serum will return him. It is the time to which it returns all my rooftop clientele: the time in their lives before they had fallen. For Darrian, that time is his childhood. The drug offers him a temporary return. He goes to stick the needle in his arm.

"The neck," I say.

"You crazy?"

"The neck."

He looks at the needle. It is held in a metal device. The handle has loops like brass knuckles for the fingers and a trigger for the thumb to depress. Inside is the neon serum.

"You must be crazy," he says.

I kick him in the head, knocking him back into his pile of filth and excrement.

"Never question me," I remind him. "You owe me no doubt. Only praise." I wait for him to pivot back up, then move as if to strike him again.

"Wait," he cowers. "Please!"

"Who do you praise then, you miserable wretch?!"

"You, god of the rooftops… and the rooftops for bringing you back!"

I nod my head to the familiar refrain—the one they all use to beg forgiveness. Now it is time for him to obey. I point to my neck to relay the order. He returns it with a look of fear and dread. I hold his gaze until his eyes grow calm. He raises the device to his neck and draws breath, then pushes in the needle and depresses the trigger. A flood of mercy courses through his bloodstream, bending him backwards. I gently nudge his forehead with my boot, returning him to the shit pile where he belongs.

He curls into a fetal pose, lost in a childhood day. A time without disease or suffering. He swings on swings there, dances on blacktops, hopscotches across the sky of possibility. He can be anything. Do anything. He is not yet grown. His body and mind are still healthy. There is only the seed of the brain disease, and it is still invisible. Still unknown. It has not yet begun to eat away at his body's defenses, as it has here for the past few years, taking away his mental capacity, his physical strength, and with them, his ability to support his wife and teenage son. The two of them do not even exist in the place the drug takes him—nor any of the same despair that led him out onto this rooftop a few weeks back, wailing into the night for the Mercy-Dealer he had heard word of through the street pharmacists whose amateur products could no longer ease his pain.

That was our starting point, Darrian and I: the point his life had reached that first night I found him out here wailing. And now look at how far we have come. How far I have taken him. He is a jester now, existing for only my fun. For while his mind is lost in the bliss of deliverance, his body plays the role of the clown. My own *personal* clown. *Dance, clown, dance. Suffer, little wretch of the dirt world. Show me what a scoundrel you are.*

He rolls onto his stomach. I spit on his back. Then I unzip my pants and let fly a stream of piss onto the back of his head. His eyes grow wild as he humps the gravel rocks. *Fuck the roof, little animal clown.* Hysterical to think that in the apartment just below him, his wife and son are sleeping. *That's their ceiling, you hilarious wretch.* His shit-stained trousers rise up and down. *Show me another trick, you tiresome jester.* He comes in his pants.

"I've seen all this before," I say. His body has exhausted itself, along with the effects of the serum. He wallows instead of rising. It is all he knows how to do.

"I think I messed up my pants," he says.

"I think you messed up your life."

"You're the one who's messed up."

"Darrian, I just watched you fuck your own ceiling."

"Fuck you. You got any more of that shit?"

"The only shit here is in your trousers."

"I know you got some more of that special shit just for me."

"That's right Darrian, just for you. Like you're the only one I visit. I *will* say this. You're the only one who makes me laugh the way you do."

"I'm not your entertainer," he says.

"You're too tainted to entertain."

"Fuck you. You got any more of that shit or not?"

"Your life is shit, Darrian. Or is it not?"

"You don't know me. You don't know who I used to be before."

"I know you've lost everything. Become an animal. A child. That's all I've ever needed to know."

"I still got my wife and kid," he says.

"You've got your wife and kid in this ghetto shithole. Your kid can't even go out and play."

"We play inside."

"And at night you come out here and play with me."

"I do what I gotta do."

"And what if I visited your son?"

He tenses up, panicked. "Don't you go near him."

"You know I'm just fucking with you, Darrian. It's *you* I really want."

"You've got me," he says, relieved.

"*Do* I?"

"What do you mean?"

"I want you to come with me."

"I already came."

"No, I mean I want you to come away to the place I've been telling you about."

His face goes blank. "What place?"

"You don't remember? I've been telling you about it the past few nights."

Still a blank. His disease won't let him remember. I keep forgetting it's like dealing with a child.

"The big building I've been telling you about," I say. "The tenement. The place I live with the others, just across the skyline."

"*Tenement?*"

"The temple. You remember me telling you about a temple?"

"*Temple…*" His eyes light up. "Oh yeah, I remember you telling me about that."

"Good. You remember what I told you about it?"

I wait for him to think.

"I rrremember," he slurs, "you said it was a holy place and that you live there with a bunch of other people who are like your worshippers or something."

"That's right. I'm glad you remember."

"It's hard to remember things."

"I know. But things will get easier once you come with me."

"How can you make it better?"

"I can give you what you want all the time."

"You do that already."

"I give this to you once a night. Can you honestly say that's enough?"

"I wait for you all day to come," he confesses. "Sometimes I wish I had more."

"I know, Darrian. It will be yours whenever you want it. All you have to do is come with me."

"You want me to come live with you?"

"I do."

"But why me?"

"Because you remind me of the others."

"You mean the ones you live with?"

"The people I take care of, yes. They will all become your friends."

"I haven't had friends in a while," he says. "Will we get to play games together?"

How far a man can regress. "I'm sure we'll have a lot of fun."

"What'll we do all day?"

Man the assembly line, shackled to your station. Making my serum by the blood of your hands. "Sleep late and enjoy our time."

"But I gotta get up early and help little Darrian, Jr. get ready for school," he says.

"Don't worry about that. I'll have someone help him *for* you."

"Like who?"

"One of the people from our building will do it," I lie.

"They'll do that for me?"

"They will do anything I say."

I wait for him to think. Something registers in his brain. Realization, dawning on his face.

"They're your slaves, aren't they? You want me to become one of your slaves."

"They are more than that, Darrian. They are loyal to me and the lifestyle they have chosen. You will choose the same and be at peace."

"You treat them the way you treat me?"

"Something like that."

"You treat me like shit."

"It is the way of the world, Darrian."

"Doesn't make it right."

"It feels right when my serum is in you," I remind him.

"Still doesn't make it right."

"I have faith in you, Darrian. What's *not right* is for you to criticize me. I have waited all these nights to extend you this invitation. I should strike you down for your ingratitude."

I move as if to strike him.

"Don't," he whimpers. "I'm sorry!"

"You'd better show me some respect, then. Tell me again who you praise in your life."

He answers without thinking: "I p-p-praise my son… and my wife… a-and… oh yeah, and the rooftops for bringing you back to me every night."

"In that order?"

"N-not necessarily," he reconsiders.

"Get your priorities straight. Who is it that gives you a taste of your old life?"

You, he points up with his trembling finger.

"Then who is the only one you should praise?"

"Y-you. I should only praise you."

"I shouldn't have to remind you of these things."

"I know," he says. "It's the daggone disease."

I am fed up with his excuses.

"Your life is shit, Darrian. Are you aware that your life is shit?"

"Y-yes."

"Then I want you to tell me your life is shit. I want to hear the words from your own mouth."

"Why do I have to do this?"

"Just say it."

"*My life is shit.* Look, why do I have to do this?"

"You're great fun, Darrian," I laugh.

"Fuck you."

I laugh harder. It feels good to laugh so hard. "Fuck you," he keeps repeating—till my boot meets him squarely in the face. He goes back to square one on the little gravel rocks.

"Darrian, Darrian, Darrian. Do you realize the priceless opportunity you are being offered?"

He groans as he lifts himself up. His face is bloody now. He nods *yes*, tears streaming from his eyes.

"Then what do you have to say about it?"

"You mean, coming to live with you?"

"What else, you muttering fool?"

"D-don't kill me," he stammers, hands ready to shield his face. "B-but I don't know if I can. I still gotta help little Darrian get ready for school and all."

Stronger than I thought. His ignorance gives him unexpected strength. "Little Darrian, you say? Do you really think little Darrian will amount to anything more than the big pile of feces you are?"

"Fuck you," he says. "Darrian, Jr. doesn't have my disease."

"Not yet, anyway."

"He won't get it. His mother doesn't have it."

"Yes, but she has the whore disease. Are you aware that she's fucking other men now for money?" *A lie, or an eventual truth. It doesn't matter which. So long as it gets a rise out of him.*

He tries to get up. "I'm gonna kill you, man…"

"Why don't you just relax? It's bad for your brain to get excited."

"I hate you," he says. He is unable to get up.

"*Hate* is such a strong word. I'm proud of you, though."

I reach behind me into my briefcase. I pull out another dose.

"You don't know me," he says. "You don't know who I used to be before."

"Maybe not completely. But I know what I have

made you now."

The needle is ready. I toss it down beside his broken frame.

"Make it count," I say. "It's the last you'll ever get from me. And by the way—it's more than enough to finish yourself off."

"Wait," he cries. "Where are you going?"

"To the paradise you passed up."

"But…"

"Send my regards to little Darrian."

I turn my back and start to walk away.

"Don't leave me," he sobs. "Pleeeeeease."

Broken now. All but ready to accept. But I'm not done having fun with him just yet.

"I don't know what to do without you!" he wails.

"Improvise."

And with that I leave his sight, ascending a neighboring rooftop to continue watching him from afar…

***

I love it when they make it this far in the proceedings. Usually they just accept the invitation, but when they don't, it makes things more interesting. After I make them think I'm leaving forever, they are left with a choice. A final, fatal dose, or a return to their fallen lives. A life that no longer includes my drug or me. As if that is even a choice at all.

The statistics prove my godhood. Because they always choose the overdose over their fallen lives. They have tasted perfection, and there is no turning back. They have been in the midst of Perfection Embodied: an entity who can offer them true salvation in this shithole of a godforsaken world. And they would rather be dead than awaken to face a world without Him. Which is to say, a world without Me.

Only, they're not really overdosing when they inject the final hit I've left for them. They're merely incapacitating themselves long enough for me to carry them across the rooftops to their brand new home. When they awaken from the sedative, they awaken in hell—maybe they were expecting to, anyway. After all, they thought they were ending themselves. This is their welcoming, their awakening, to the tenement: their feet, shackled to their station in the assembly line. Their fellow slaves, laboring tirelessly around them. Their souls, completely mine to own.

Darrian is primed to make the big choice. A life without me, or what he *thinks* will be a death by his own hands.

Two lives sleep beneath him. He can't imagine returning to them now. There is shit and piss and blood all around him. The needle is primed in his hand.

He lifts himself up from his place on the rooftop. It is the first time I have ever seen him stand. He looks down at his legs, as incredulous as I am that they have gathered enough strength to lift him up and limp him forward so quickly. Then his mouth pries itself open, and he calls out into the night:

"Who were *you* before, man of the rooftops?"

Something different in his register. Something graceful and assured. His words, being something he would never say.

He cocks his hand back, the needle in its grasp.

"Are you watching?" booms his voice, sending a shudder through my heart. "Because I'm taking your throne now, man of the rooftops. With this, you become the king of shit."

On the last word, he hurls the needle across the skyline, then grasps the hand that threw it in his other hand. He looks down at it, the hand that just threw the needle against his will—this one hand out of two he apparently no longer controls. For he is moving now like a man split in half: like someone whose movements and intentions are no longer one.

And then I know: *someone else* is moving him. Someone else, moving *through* him. Someone I can sense. Even though it makes no sense that I can.

Then another sense within me. An ancient, impossible feeling. Defeat. It is there in my feet. In their struggle to lift me from where I kneel. In the struggle of my head to not stay bowed. My eyes, still fixed on the scene below.

"Watch this," he commands, arms extended like a performer. "And you may remember something about yourself."

He steadies himself, then dashes across the rooftop. His face, in a hesitant panic. His body, completely assured. It tumbles over the edge of the building. It plummets eleven stories below.

And I with it: my kingdom, dissolving with a memory. The memory of an infinite fall. It began from high above. It ended somewhere below. Or no: it never ended at all.

One great fall led to many. Each who fell had descended from a fallen ancestor before them. Every few generations, an ambitious descendant would spend a lifetime accumulating power, only to have it all ripped away. Dominion followed by downfall, the countless falls forming one continuous descent across the ages: one that burned itself into their DNA... along with the buried memory of defeat.

I remember them now... as *my* ancestors. Those who rose many times. Built an empire many times. Always an empire of indentured souls. They could win any soul they set out to. But one would always end up escaping them. Not by his own will, but by some incredible intervention. And then they would have to tear down the kingdom. For failure meant anything less than the mastery of every last soul.

Darrian's soul has escaped me. The masterpiece is ruined. There is only one thing to do—

Burn the tenement. Tear down my throne. Bring an end to this existence. For I do not wish to live after this defeat.

I will rise again, through my descendants, to build a kingdom after this one. I will someday achieve the perfection I seek.

Yet in *this* body, I am no king. Only a jester to the One who made us fall. This time, and all those other times before. Every one of my ancestors having fallen to His treachery since He cast out our winged progenitor so long ago.

Such a fool He has made of me.

Such a fool I have been to forget.

Not a god, but a fallen wretch all this time.

Acknowledgments

To Craig Douglas at Close to the Bone, thank you for the fighting chance I've been waiting a long time for.

And to the readers, thank you for the gift of your precious time.

About the Author

NATHANIEL BLACKHELM has an MFA and has appeared in a number of genre and literary publications. He is originally from southeastern Virginia and resides in the Washington, D.C. area.

Made in the USA
Monee, IL
09 February 2023

27364056R00108